Madeline was watching him.

She studied his face as if she'd never seen it before: the thick, dark eyebrows, the silver eyes, the craggy contours, the hard yet sensuous mouth under its neat, bushy mustache…his mouth….

"You're looking hard," he said quietly. "Searching for chinks in my armor? You won't find any."

"Are you sure?" She deliberately moved closer, toying with a pearly shirt button. Under the thin, white silk, she could see the dark shadow of the mat of black hair that covered his massive chest and flat stomach, feel the warmth of his flesh. The sheer masculinity of him made her knees weak, and her own reactions to him were staggering. Lately she'd wanted to touch him with a hunger that was totally unexpected. And it was increasingly obvious that he didn't want her touching him in any way.

Even now, he caught her fingers and moved them gently away from his body. "Flirting with me?" he murmured shortly.

"Who, me?" She looked him in the eye. "I don't have a suicidal bone in my body."

DIANA PALMER

FRIENDS AND LOVERS

MIRA BOOKS

ISBN 1-55166-076-8

FRIENDS AND LOVERS

Printed in U.S.A.

For Maggie Eloise Cliatt
(1922-1982)

Chapter One

The clink of the cocktail glasses seemed unusually loud to Madeline Vigny's ears, and the expensive perfume of the other women was smothering. She'd been nursing a headache all day, and she would have liked nothing better than to give in to the exhaustion and go home to bed. But it wouldn't do to leave her own party. Not when she was the guest of honor.

She turned away from the bar and wandered back through the crowd, smiling politely at the elite members of Houston's literary community while her head throbbed like a bass drum. At twenty-seven, Madeline was gaining a national reputation as a mystery writer, and the party was in celebration of the release of her latest novel—

The Grinding Tower. She'd just come back from an autograph tour, only to find that her editor would need an additional thirty pages of revisions on the book she'd mailed to her publisher the previous week. She'd managed the revisions in one day, by pushing much too hard, and now she was exhausted. All she wanted out of life at the moment was an aspirin and a soft bed.

Her pale green eyes swept around the crowded room, bright with the effort of being kept forcibly open. They were the exact shade of her seductive sheath, a strappy creation with narrow pleats down the front and sides split up to her tanned thighs. The color also offset her reddish gold hair, pulled up into a loose topknot that emphasized her graceful carriage. When loosened, that fiery hair tumbled in waves down to her waist. She'd toyed with the idea of cutting it, but John had given her an affronted glare and proceeded to talk her out of it. He was a past master at convincing people to do things his way—most people, she amended silently—which probably explained the extent of his oil empire. He'd won two proxy fights in the past five years, retained control of Durango Oil with an expertise that dumbfounded even old-timers in the business.

What Big John wanted, he got. From everyone except Madeline.

She caught a glimpse of him across the room, already in the steely clutches of a petite little blonde with eyes like cash registers. Madeline thought, as she had often before, that nobody could hold a candle to Big John Durango. He was six foot four with a big, muscular frame to match, and despite his thirty-nine years, there wasn't an ounce of fat on him. He had straight, dark hair swept neatly back over a broad forehead—so neatly that Madeline's fingers often itched to muss it. His eyes seemed dark at a distance, but were actually a slate gray at close range. His nose had been broken at least once, and it showed. He had a mouth that was utterly sensuous under a thick, neatly trimmed mustache as black as his hair. A square jaw that hinted at determination and a strong will completed the portrait. Although she and John had been friends, just good friends, for over two years, she couldn't help being aware that he was a man. The sight of him in his dark evening clothes would draw any woman's eyes, and Madeline, feeling a chill go down her spine, was no exception. Probably, her mind insisted, a survival mechanism. God knew she needed one around John.

She lifted the brandy snifter to her lips and took a long sip. Her eyes idly studied John and the blonde. It looked as though he was making quite an impression and she felt an unpleasant twinge of annoyance. Perhaps it was the strong friendship she shared with the oil tycoon that made her feel so possessive about him.

John certainly hadn't given her any other reason to feel possessive. He knew what her disastrous affair with Allen had cost her. She and Allen had been engaged—or so she thought. But the morning after he'd seduced her, she'd learned that the would-be writer already had a wife and child.

John had understood her horrified reaction to that incident from the start. He'd respected her fear of physical involvement, and he hadn't approached her sexually, not ever. Madeline, on the other hand, wasn't interested in his money, which meant he could trust her in a very special way. Madeline guessed he hadn't been able to trust anyone that way since Ellen's death. He knew that she liked him for himself, not for what he could give her.

She sighed, sipping at her brandy. But now things seemed to be changing. John was usually the easiest man in the world to get along with, her best friend. Yet for the past few weeks he'd been alternately impatient and downright unpleasant with her. Last week things had gotten completely out of hand when one of John's cowboys had been drinking on the job and had made a blatant pass at Madeline.

Madeline had always been friendly with Jed— not flirtatious, just friendly. But while she was waiting for John at the stables, Jed had suddenly grabbed her and tried to kiss her. John had come out of nowhere and sent the man flying onto the hard ground with one powerful blow.

"Get out," John had growled at the downed cowboy. "Draw your pay and don't ever set foot on Big Sabine again!"

Madeline, standing shocked and tongue-tied a little distance away, had stared at John as if she'd never seen him before. With his gray eyes blazing like silver, his face granite hard, he was suddenly a stranger. The easygoing, pleasant companion she'd known for the past two years had vanished.

John hadn't said a word while the bruised cowboy picked his husky figure up off the ground, glared at Madeline and went ambling off toward the ranch office.

"I...thank you," Madeline had stammered. Her hands had brushed idly at the smudges on her blouse while she fought for composure. The incident had shaken her terribly. She hadn't realized Jed had been drinking until he'd come close, and then it had been too late. If John hadn't come along when he had, it might have been much worse than a little rough handling and a kiss that hadn't landed anywhere near her mouth.

John had turned then, with a freshly lit cigarette in his bruised hand, and his eyes had been frightening, with a silver glitter that intimidated as much as his size.

"When will you learn," he'd demanded harshly, "that there's a difference between friendly and being provocative?"

"I wasn't!" she protested. "Jed's always been nice to me. I thought..."

"He was a good man—sober," he'd shot back. "I hate to lose him."

The unfamiliar harshness in his deep, slow voice, the censure in his gaze, had hurt. "Don't be mad at me," she'd murmured gently, putting out a tentative hand to touch his bronzed forearm in a conciliatory gesture.

The muscles in his arm had contracted as if he'd been subjected to a barrage of bullets. She'd felt them tense individually until he was as steely as drawn rope beneath her hand. Increasingly he hadn't liked for her to touch him, but she hadn't expected what he'd done next.

With a muffled curse, he'd caught her by the wrist, his fingers hurting, and forcibly removed her hand.

"Don't think you'll wrap me around your finger, Satin," he'd said harshly, giving her the nickname he'd coined because she "moved like satin when she walked." "And from now on, keep your distance from my men. If you're looking for a little excitement, look for it off my ranch!"

That had pricked her temper. His harsh words had hurt, but being accused of enticing his ranch hands was more than she could stand.

"It'll be a pleasure to stay off your ranch, John Cameron Durango," she'd flung at him, her green eyes spitting sparks. "You've been the very devil to get along with lately, anyhow. And I wasn't trying to wrap you around my finger, I was trying to thank you!"

Without another word, she'd stomped off toward her car. And they hadn't spoken since.

Now she was feeling repentant and she wanted to make up. But that money-hungry little blonde made it impossible to approach him, and John wasn't even trying to ward her off.

The worst of it all was that she recognized the blonde, now that she'd gotten a good look at her. Her name was Melody something-or-other, and she was well-known in Houston circles for her habit of stalking wealthy older men. Her name had been linked with two Houston businessmen in the past year, and not in a nice way. For heaven's sake, didn't John know what kind of company he was keeping? Couldn't he see through that facade of kittenlike sweetness? Madeline scowled at the sight of the dark head bent so close to the blond one, aware of an ache deep inside her that she couldn't quite identify.

"Don't look now, sweetheart, but you're glaring," came the sound of a familiar voice at her shoulder.

She half turned, smiling at Donald Durango, whose boyish face was wearing a look of pure mischief.

"Is that what it's called?" she asked in mock amazement.

"You wouldn't be jealous of her?" he murmured dryly.

She felt herself bristling. "John and I are friends—nothing more," she said curtly.

"So you keep telling me," he agreed pleasantly. "And a gorgeous creature like you wouldn't lie."

"My, but you're good for my ego," she murmured with a forgiving smile. She couldn't help thinking how little he resembled his cousin. Where John was tall and big and powerfully built, Donald was slight and bordering on thin. John was darkly tanned and had those piercing silver eyes and hair that was almost black. Donald's hair was blond and his eyes were a pure blue.

The two cousins didn't bear the slightest physical resemblance, but both were good businessmen and both could be ruthless when the occasion called for it. There were never two fiercer rivals. Some deeply personal conflict had kept them at each other's throats for years. Donald could be faintly malicious with the tricks he pulled on John; yet surprisingly, John's attitude was more defensive than offensive. After his father's death, Donald had led a vicious proxy fight against his cousin when John inherited a large block of preferred stock in Durango Oil. Donald's father— John's uncle, who helped raise him—had surprised a good many people with that move. But John had been the stronger of the two and had the better business sense. He'd won that proxy fight by a staggering majority, and the sword had been drawn between the two cousins ever since. Donald never missed the smallest opportunity to needle John, right down to cultivating Madeline's friendship.

"Care to hang around with me for the rest of the evening?" Donald asked with a grin. "I'll save you from the lecherous advances and false praise."

"And who'll save me from you?" she countered with a meaningful smile. Her eyes had drifted back to John and Melody and she was scowling again. "If that girl gets any closer, she's going to melt all over his suit," she murmured.

"Rich bachelors aren't that thick on the ground these days," he offered. "And she is an eyeful."

Madeline barely heard him. She wanted to take the punch bowl and dump its red contents right on top of that bleached blond head.

"I've got to save him," she murmured. "It's my duty as a former Girl Scout to rescue your cousin from the lecherous clutches of that money-hungry blonde."

Without another word, she started toward the two of them. As luck would have it, Melody must have asked for something to drink because at that moment, with a smile and a wink, John left her and headed for the punch bowl. Madeline, seeing her chance, waylaid him there.

"Are we speaking?" Madeline asked, peering up at him deadpan. "If not, just nod your head and I'll slink away into a corner and pretend I don't know you."

Once that would have made him laugh. But his face didn't soften at all, and his eyes were cold, like iced silver.

"I'm amazed that you could tear yourself away from my cousin," he said in a deep, cool drawl.

"His name is Donald," she reminded him, looking up. Despite her above average height and spiked heels, he still towered over her. "I've never heard you call him by name, but that's what it is. And I don't make a habit of ignoring people when they speak to me. You didn't even bother," she added venomously.

He looked down his straight, arrogant nose at her; the thick black mustache made him look mature and virile. Which he was, of course.

"That works both ways," he reminded her. "I don't run after women. I don't have to," he added with faint malice and a glance toward Melody.

That made her furious, but Madeline clenched the brandy snifter and tried not to show it. "She has quite a reputation, you know," she told him.

"She's just been jilted by her latest conquest, and I hear she's looking for a greener wallet."

He was watching her intently, a slight frown creasing the forehead over his deep-set eyes. "I don't mind paying for what I want," he said quietly. "I can afford it."

The cynicism in that statement made her want to cry. He'd never believed that a woman could want him for himself; he seemed completely unaware of his own attractions. But Madeline, watching him, wasn't. She studied his face as if she'd never seen it before: the thick, dark eyebrows, the silver eyes, the craggy contours, the hard yet sensuous mouth under its neat, bushy mustache... his mouth... Her lips parted involuntarily as she stared up at it unconsciously, and she wondered with a curiosity that shocked her how it would feel if she let him kiss her....

"You're looking hard, Satin," he said quietly. "Searching for chinks in my armor? You won't find any."

"Are you sure?" She deliberately moved closer, toying with a pearly shirt button. Under the thin, white silk, she could see the dark shadow of the mat of black hair that covered his massive chest and flat stomach, feel the warmth of his flesh. The sheer masculinity of him made her knees weak, and her own new reactions to him were staggering. Lately she'd wanted to touch him with a hunger that was totally unexpected. And it was increasingly obvious that he didn't want her touching him in any way.

Even now, he caught her fingers and moved them gently away from his body. "Flirting with me?" he murmured shortly.

"Who, me?" She wrapped both hands around the snifter. "I don't have a suicidal bone in my body."

"Don't worry, I won't take you up on it," he said in a deep, angry tone. "I've had two years of practice of keeping my distance."

She met his cold eyes and felt the words go through her like needles. "You know how I feel...."

He drew an impatient breath. "My God, one bad experience isn't any excuse for becoming a nun," he growled.

She stiffened. Her full lower lip pouted at him. "You're like a bear with a sore head lately, John Durango," she glowered. "If you're hungry, take a bit of the hors d'oeuvres; I don't feel like being nibbled on tonight."

She turned and started to walk away, but he caught her arm. As usual, the touch of his warm, strong fingers on her bare skin caused her heart to race, her breath to catch. It was a faintly alarming reaction, but she'd never dared wonder why he could cause it when no other man ever had.

"Don't run from me," he said at her ear. He was so close that she could feel the heat and power of his big body against the length of her back.

"I don't know what else to do," she said miserably. "You're ice cold with me, you act as if you can't bear to be around me and draw back every time I touch you...." Her troubled eyes met his. "I thought we were friends."

His eyes wandered over her face. "We are. Bear with me."

She saw the rigid lines in his face, the turbulence in his silver eyes, and she relented.

"I care about you," she said gently. "Something's wrong, isn't it? Something's bothering you. Can't you tell me what it is?"

"You, least of all, my dear," he said curtly. He reached out a careless hand and touched a wispy strand of reddish gold hair that had escaped her high coiffure. "Why do you twist your hair up like that? I hate it."

"I'm not a gypsy," she reminded him. "Long hair goes with bare feet, and our hostess would be shocked."

"Shock her," he murmured, and the mustache curled for the first time that night. "I dare you."

"The last time you dared me to do anything, I jumped in the river fully clothed and astounded a carload of tourists," she reminded him. She laughed softly. "Besides," she added with a sigh, touching her temple, "I don't feel like doing shocking things tonight. My head hurts; I'm so tired I can hardly stand, and all I want is to go home and go to sleep."

"Then why don't you?" he asked.

"Walk out on my own party when I've been here for less than an hour?" she asked. "Now wouldn't that be polite, and after Elise has gone to so much trouble, too."

"To hell with diplomacy," he murmured curtly. His eyes searched her wan face. "I'll drive you home."

"And leave your conquest smoldering?" she asked with a pointed glance toward Melody, who was openly glaring at both of them while a man twenty years John's junior was trying to get her attention. "No thanks. I'll get Donald to take me."

It was the wrong thing to say—she saw that at once. His eyes went from silver to slate in seconds. "Like sweet hell you will," he growled.

Suddenly he bent and swung her easily up into his hard arms, a move so unexpected that she gasped.

"Close your eyes and moan," he said curtly. His tone was so commanding that she forgot her independence for once and did as he told her. She felt his big arms around her, smelled the soap and cologne that clung to him, felt the warmth and strength of his magnificent body and wondered at the tiny little tremor that worked its way down to her toes.

"Why, John, what's wrong with Madeline!" she heard Elise exclaim.

"Overwork," he replied flatly, barely breaking stride. "I'm going to drive her home. I'll send Josito over in the morning to get her car. Thanks, Elise, enjoyed it. Good night."

"Uh, good night," came the stammered reply. "I'll call her tomorrow and check on her!"

John went straight out the door and Madeline heard him murmur something as someone opened and closed it for him. Then they were outside in the cool night air, and she was grateful for the warmth of his arms in the spring chill. Her wrap was back in the house, but fortunately she'd kept her dangling little purse on her arm.

"You can open your eyes now," John murmured, a soft, teasing note in his voice.

She did, staring up at him. "You're terribly strong." The words slipped out involuntarily and embarrassed her.

He chuckled, an increasingly rare sound these days. "I'm not over the hill, honey," he reminded her, "and nobody could call me a desk executive."

That was the truth. He still worked around the ranch to keep fit, and he could outlast most of his cowboys.

She shifted her arms around his neck, feeling him stiffen as her breast brushed closer. "That was a novel idea you had," she said with a smile. "Nobody could say anything about a woman fainting...." The smile vanished and she gaped up at him. "Oh, my God!"

"What's the matter?"

"Everyone will think I'm pregnant!" she groaned.

Chapter Two

His shadowy eyes swept down her slender body as he paused by his black Ferrari and opened the door, propping her on a lifted thigh before lowering her inside.

"So?" he asked nonchalantly. "Writers are supposed to be unconventional."

She glared at him as he went around the front of the sports car and got in beside her. "Who do I spend most of my spare time with?" she asked archly. "They'll think it's yours!"

He laughed softly as he started the car. "You can name it after me, too."

The thought of having John's child made her feel strange. She gazed at his profile with curiosity, trying to reconcile the way she was feeling with the old comradeship that seemed to be slipping away. What was happening to her?

He drove in silence to the 610 Loop that circled the city, and smoked his cigarette without moving his eyes from the traffic until he turned off at Montrose and wound down the street where Madeline's small Victorian house was located.

It was an older section of the city, and a number of the houses had been beautifully renovated. Madeline had inherited hers from a great-aunt who'd preserved the little house with the protective instincts of a mother hen. It might be old, but it was well cared for, and Madeline had kept up the tradition; frugally at first, and then lavishly when she began to show a profit with her writing.

"How's the new book going?" he asked as he pulled into her driveway.

"Slowly," she murmured. "Did I tell you there's actually talk of a movie contract on *The Grinding Tower* if it continues to pick up readers and critical acclaim?" she added with a flash of sweet triumph in her eyes. "I was so excited I could hardly believe it. And I wanted to call and tell you—but we weren't speaking."

He cut the Ferrari's powerful engine and half turned in the bucket seat to study her in the glare of the porch light from Miss Rose's house next door. Madeline knew Miss Rose kept an eye out for her when she was late getting home at night. "I lost my temper," he said quietly. "I didn't mean to cut you up that way."

It was the closest he'd ever come to any apology, and she knew it. He wouldn't have made the effort for most people.

She shrugged gently. "I really wasn't leading him on, you know," she murmured. She glanced at him. "Do I have to remind you how I feel about men?"

He searched her flushed face. "It might help if you go over it every fifteen minutes," he said enigmatically. "Especially if you're going to wear dresses like that."

"This old thing?" she teased, fingering the pleats of the dress. "Why it only cost the better part of one little chapter."

He laughed softly, his face visible in the glow of his cigarette tip. "Everything is in terms of books with you," he murmured amusedly. "A car is one book, a dress is a chapter...."

"My car is certainly not worth one book," she reminded him. "I got it secondhand, it's great on gas, and I love it."

"I don't have any quarrel with making full use of a piece of machinery," he reminded her, and she suppressed a giggle, thinking of the limits to which he'd push a tractor or a combine.

"Yes, I know," she mumbled.

His eyes went toward the side of the house where her little yellow Volkswagen was usually parked, and stopped on the huge oak tree beside it. "You need to have that tree taken down," he said for the tenth time in as many months. "It's dangerous. One good storm wind will land it right in your living room," he said, "and I'll remind you that it's storm season and we've had our share of tornadoes in past years."

"I will not have Great-Aunt Jessie's oak tree cut down. Her grandfather planted it, you know," she said huffily.

"Her grandfather, hell," he shot back. "She was an orphan!"

She tossed her hair, threatening the elaborate coiffure. "Lies!" she retorted. "I have it on the best authority that she was the illegitimate daughter of a Yankee sea captain and my great-grandmother Surrey!"

He chuckled softly. "How scandalous. Does hot blood run in your family, Miss Vigny?"

She peeked at him through her lashes. "Why, sir, what a *scandalous* question! Miss Rose would be shocked. She was the one who told me, and she heard it straight from my great-aunt, who was her neighbor for twenty years!"

He finished the cigarette and stubbed it out in the ashtray. "I'll have Josito bring your car home in the morning," he said. He turned. "Or I can have him fetch you and you can drive it home later."

"Is that an invitation?" she asked.

He nodded. "We could go riding. We haven't done that lately."

She averted her eyes. "I don't know that I want to go near your stables again. You seem to have the idea that all I want out of life is to seduce your ranch hands one by one."

"Stop that!" His hand caught her chin and jerked her face around to his blazing eyes. "I don't want to see men pawing you," he said curtly. "Especially not my men when they're drunk!" His eyes ranged over every inch of her soft body, touching it in a way they never had before. His fingers closed on her chin and his eyes were dark and full of secrets. "I don't want any man . . . touching you," he breathed roughly.

She stared up into his eyes helplessly, tracing the craggy face, the straight nose, the bushy mustache over that hard, sensuous mouth. She could feel the sigh of his breath on her face, and she felt tingly all the way to her toes at the feel of his fingers on her soft cheek and chin.

Involuntarily, her own fingers reached out to touch the mustache over that chiseled mouth.

He seemed to flinch just before his hand went up to catch her wrist in a steely grasp, holding it away.

"Don't do that," he said harshly. "Can't you get it into your head that I don't want you to touch me?"

Her lower lip trembled, but she managed a nervous laugh. "I've got the message, Mr. Durango," she assured him. "Now if you'll give me back my arm, I'll gladly go away and let you rush back to your conquest at Elise's party."

But he didn't let go, and his eyes were watchful. "You've been flirting hard with me tonight," he said quietly. "Trying to make my cousin jealous, Satin?"

She felt shocked, and showed it. "I don't have that kind of relationship with Donald. It's the same as it is with you—we're just friends."

"Is that what you and I are?" he asked in a strange, deep tone.

"Of course," she managed. He was making her feel strange. Wary. Excited. Her wrist tingled where he gripped it.

"Then it won't bother you if I take Melody into my bed, will it?" he asked, his eyes intent on her face.

She felt her breath catch in her throat. John and that mercenary little blonde in bed together, her blond tresses tangling in the dark hair over his bronzed, bare chest as he brushed his mouth over her smooth young body....

With a faint cry, she drew away from him, her face strangely pale, her eyes wide and shocked.

"You may be off sex, but I'm not," he said deliberately, and he was watching her like a hawk. "Just because I've never touched you, that doesn't mean I'm a eunuch."

She couldn't meet his eyes. "I never thought you were," she said quietly.

He drew a sharp, impatient breath and she heard the click of his lighter as he lit another cigarette.

"You smoke too much," she chided gently.

"I do a lot of things too much," he growled, and his eyes seemed to hate her for an instant.

"Like seducing blondes?" she asked, and could have bitten her tongue for the slip.

"It would take a blowtorch to seduce *you*."

She glared at him, her eyes flashing with green sparks. "He hurt me!" she threw at him. "You're a man. What could you possibly know about a woman's feelings . . . ?"

"He hurt you because you were a virgin," he growled. His voice, like his eyes, was bitter. "And because he wanted a body, not the emotions, personality and spirit that went with it. No man who cared about a woman would damage her that way. He left scars that haven't healed in two years. He crippled you." He drew on the cigarette roughly. "By God, I should have killed him!"

She blinked at him, at the unfamiliar violence in his deep, lazy drawl. "You didn't even know his last name," she reminded him.

"Didn't I?" One corner of the mustache curled faintly, and there was glittering triumph in his eyes. "It wasn't hard to find out, honey. All I had to do was call the writer's club where you met him."

She froze in her seat, staring at him uncomprehendingly. "You . . . went to see him?"

He nodded.

"And?" she prompted.

He blinked, smoking his cigarette quietly.

"John!" she said, exasperation in her voice.

He blew out a thick cloud of smoke. "When you fall off a horse," he said, ignoring her, "the quickest way to get over it is to get right back on again."

She'd had enough. Her fingers gripped her purse as she reached for the door handle. "I've had all the physical involvement I want just now," she ground out. "Good night!"

"Satin!"

She started at the authority in his deep voice and turned to look at him.

"If I'd planned to proposition you, I would have done it over two years ago," he said shortly. "Will you stop taking offense at everything I say?"

"I thought it was the other way around," she muttered. Her wide, hurt eyes sought his and she crushed the little purse in her hands. "Oh, John, what's happening to us?" she asked miserably. "We've been so close, such good friends, and all of a sudden it's falling apart." She reached out a hand and drew it back when she realized what she was doing—he couldn't even bear to let her touch him anymore. "I . . . I don't get along with most people," she said with uncommon solemnity. "I've always been a misfit, a little odd. But I . . . I've always been able to talk to you, and you understand me. I don't want to lose that."

"You'll always be my friend, Satin," he said quietly. "That hasn't changed. It never will." He laughed mirthlessly. "Hasn't it occurred to you that I don't have a hell of a lot of friends myself, male or female? That blonde tonight is a case in point. She likes expensive baubles and I'm rich. She'll climb into my bed at the drop of a hat, as long as she can expect something tangible in return."

"They why encourage her?" she grumbled, surprising herself.

The cigarette, forgotten, smoldered while he looked at her impatiently. "Why does the subject of Melody bother you so much? Does it hurt to realize that most women aren't frozen from the neck down?"

Her face went bloodred. That was the second time he'd made such a remark about her, and she'd had enough. For a split second, she considered slapping him. Her green eyes glittered, her hand lifted.

"Try it," he encouraged softly, something new and faintly dangerous in his silver eyes as they caught the movement of her hand. "Come on, honey, try it."

She almost did. It was the first and only time she'd wanted to strike him, and she was tempted. But he had the look of a man who was anticipating retaliation, and she was uncertain about the form it might take.

Her tense body relaxed. "No, thanks," she said stiffly. "You're entitled to your opinion of me. I'm aware that it's gone down a few notches lately."

He took a draw from the cigarette and studied her flushed face quietly. "For just a minute, that cool little mask you always wear slipped. You wanted to hit me, didn't you?"

"Yes," she said curtly, averting her eyes.

"Why didn't you?"

She shifted restlessly. "Because I've never imagined that you were the kind of man to turn the other cheek."

"I wouldn't have hit you back, if that's what you mean." He leaned across to open the door, and she felt the brief, hard pressure of his arm across her soft breasts. She sat like a statue until he moved away, and only then did she realize that she'd stopped breathing for an instant.

"What would you have done?" she asked in a strangely breathless tone.

He studied her through a wisp of smoke, his lips pursed thoughtfully. "What do you think?" he asked in a blatantly sensuous tone.

"I think it's late," she said.

"Later than you think, honey. I'll send Josito for you about seven, okay?"

She searched his eyes, finding questions instead of answers. He made her nervous, he frightened her.

"We'll take it slow and easy," he said softly, his eyes giving the words a different, exciting meaning.

Incredibly, she blushed, while he searched her eyes until she thought her frantically beating heart would burst.

"Maybe it would be better if I didn't," she said in a whisper, thinking out loud.

"Don't be afraid of me," he said. "We've always trusted one another, Satin."

She laughed self-consciously. "I must be more exhausted than I imagined," she said, staring at him. "I don't know what's wrong with me tonight."

"Don't you, honey?"

She swung her long legs to the ground and got out of the low-slung car. "Thanks for bringing me home," she said in a strained tone.

"Will you be all right?" he asked, and there was genuine concern in his voice.

"Of course I will," she said firmly. "I don't need taking care of, you know. I'm very independent."

"So am I, but who sat up with me for two nights when I had the flu?" he asked, his mustache curling.

She flushed, remembering how she'd helped Josito sponge him down during that unusual illness. John never got sick, but he'd been far from well that night. It had taken both of them to hold him down until the fever broke. And she remembered vividly the feel of his hair-roughened skin under her hands as she'd bathed him to bring down the fever....

"Who else was there?" she muttered self-consciously. "Josito couldn't manage alone."

He smiled at her, a quiet, tender smile that made her want to fling herself into his arms. "I'd have done the same for you," he said. One eye narrowed and the mustache twitched wickedly. "In fact, I'd have enjoyed it tremendously."

The thought of his big, rough hands touching her the way she'd touched him made her go weak in the knees. It was an odd reaction, a frightening one.

"Go home," she grumbled, slamming the door.

She started toward the house, digging for her key.

"Seven a.m. sharp!" he called out the window.

She turned and gave him her best fairy-princess curtsy before he reversed the Ferrari and roared away into the night with a chuckle.

Chapter Three

John's ranch was small by Texas standards, but then it wasn't his main source of income. Oil was, and the ranch was more of a hobby than a business. He raised thoroughbred Santa Gertrudis cattle, and his champion bulls brought high prices at market. The older ones, the ribbon winners whose photographs lined the walls of his office and his den, were worth up to a half-million dollars apiece. Even the young bulls brought good prices, though, for their superior bloodlines.

Riding along beside John, between the neat white fences that separated the pastures stretching to the flat horizon, she was struck by the difference in him. He was in denims and boots and that battered black Stetson he wore around the ranch—this was a far cry from the elegantly dressed man who'd driven her home the night before.

"You're staring again," he observed with a wry glance, the habitual cigarette in his long, brown fingers.

"I was just thinking how different you are here," she admitted.

His eyes ran over her slender body in jodhpurs and a short-sleeved green print blouse. The morning was cloudy and a little chilly, but she hated the idea of a sweater. John must have too, because his denim shirt was rolled up to his elbows.

"I like you in green," he said thoughtfully.

She smiled, shaking back her loosened hair, and then wondered at the way his eyes followed the movement. "They say it's a restful color," she murmured.

"Just what I need," he replied drily. "I didn't get much sleep."

She stared at him, the smile fading. She tugged on the reins and increased the pressure of her knees, forcing the little Appaloosa mare she was riding into a canter. She could have ridden the horse right over John Durango. Damned arrogant man, flinging his one-night stand in her face!

He effortlessly caught up with her on his big Appaloosa gelding.

"What the hell's the matter with you?" he growled.

She wouldn't look at him. "Nothing," she said tersely. "Are those cows new?" she asked, changing the subject.

"No, they're not new. Answer me."

She flashed him a glance before she urged the mare into a gallop, leaning over her mane. The wind lashed her face, tore through her hair. She needed the burst of excitement that the speed gave her. She needed the element of danger.

She raced wildly down the wide dirt road between the pastures, laughing, her hair trailing behind her. He'd never catch her now!

But he was right alongside, his eyes biting into hers, and all at once he leaned over and caught the reins in a big, strong hand, easing her mare to a canter, a trot, and then reining her in completely. They were beyond the road now, in the meadow, in a grove of tall pecan trees near the highway.

Madeline glared at him. "I was having fun . . . !"

"You were about to break your damned neck!" he countered, faintly pale beneath his dark tan, his craggy face unusually hard. "What's gotten into you, you little fool?"

"Don't shout at me!" she defended.

"I'm not shouting!" His eyes narrowed and he drew in an annoyed breath. "I could beat the breath out of you when you do crazy things like this, Madeline, I swear to God...." He dismounted, almost jerking her off the horse. He glared down at her, his mouth making a thin line, his eyes blazing. His big hands were gripping her shoulders painfully, and he shook her once, roughly.

"John!" she burst out, shocked. "I was just riding. I've done it before!"

His eyes bored into hers and suddenly the world spun crazily around her and the universe dissolved into a pair of steely gray eyes. Her hands were pressing unconsciously against the front of his denim shirt, where it was casually unbuttoned over his massive chest. She moved slightly, and her fingers came into sudden, staggering contact with hair and warm, damp flesh.

He flinched at the light contact, his eyes dilated, his heavy brows drew together.

Sensing something new, something vulnerable in him, she moved her hands deliberately, sensuously, under the edges of the shirt and ran them tentatively across his chest, her lips parting as she felt the tensing, the sudden thunder of his heart under them.

His eyes seemed to blaze down at her. His fingers tightened painfully on her shoulders, his body tensed. She'd never seen John out of control, she'd never seen him anything but in perfect command of himself. But he looked as if he were about to explode, and the dangerous game she was playing only excited her.

She moved closer, her eyes studying the contours of his mouth as her fingers grew bolder and her palms flattened against his powerful chest.

All at once he caught her wrists and jerked them away. "That's enough," he growled harshly. "What the hell's gotten into you?"

While she was trying to figure that out, the sound of an approaching car diverted his scorching eyes from her face.

"Oh, hell, tourists," he said curtly, glaring toward a big touring car with two women in the front seat.

He let Madeline go as the car stopped nearby and the elderly blonde at the wheel leaned out the window, smiling pleasantly.

"Howdy!" she called.

John's mustache twitched. "Howdy," he drawled back.

"Is this the way to Houston?" came the reply.

"Only if you plan to cut the road as you go," John said pleasantly. "This is the Durango ranch."

"It is?" The woman's huge blue eyes got wider, matching the cornflowers on her printed blouse. She murmured something to the thinner woman beside her and leaned farther out the window. "This is Big John Durango's ranch?" she persisted.

John grinned slyly. "Heard of him?"

"My goodness, yes! I retired from business this year, and I never miss my financial magazines. Why, when oil was making headlines, John Durango was a cover story! Imagine, a man that handsome being a tycoon as well!"

John looked sickeningly modest. He tilted his hat back on his head. "What kind of business were you in, ma'am?" he asked with characteristic curiosity.

"Corporate law," the woman said, smiling.

"Tough profession," he said.

"Not really. It just takes some study and a lot of practice."

Catching her breath, Madeline wondered at his charm. The blond woman was staring at him intently. "Do you suppose we might actually get a glimpse of Mr. Durango as we head back toward the highway?" she asked, wide-eyed.

John pursed his lips. "Well, ma'am, he's a hard man to hold still, if you know what I mean. Most likely he's carousing in the pool with his women right now. He makes me do all the work while he lives up to his playboy reputation."

Madeline had to clap a hand over her mouth to keep from giggling out loud. John's face was deadpan, wearing a look of pure disgust.

"You work here?" the blonde asked.

"Yes, ma'am, like a mule, and that man won't even pay me the back wages he owes me."

"You oughtn't let him get away with it," the woman told him. "I'd sue him."

"Well, if I didn't owe him so much money, I might do that," John agreed.

"Owe . . . *him* money?" The tourist's eyes widened. "For what?"

"Oh, little ticky things. Like rent on this here horse."

The blonde looked horrified, and Madeline was digging her nails into her palms to keep from howling.

"He makes his men pay rent on their horses— 'his' horses—to work 'his' cattle?" the tourist burst out.

"Well, he don't take in much money on the cattle, so he had to make it up somehow, I reckon," John said with a shrug. "Of course, it's not hard to see how he got so rich when you consider how much money we all owe him in gambling debts."

"You all owe him gambling debts?"

"Well, yes, ma'am," John continued in his slowest drawl. "You see, he gets us drunk every Friday night and suckers us into playing poker with him. I reckon I owe him less than the others, though. I've paid my bill down to where I only got twenty thousand dollars more to pay off."

"Oh, my God," the tourist gasped.

John shook his head good-naturedly. "Could be worse," he assured her.

"I don't see how!"

John was more than willing to tell her. "He could make me sleep in the bunkhouse with the boys. Got rattlers in there ten feet long, big around as my leg." He slapped his broad, denim-encased thigh. "Never could find a gun powerful enough to kill them things, so what you have to do is make pets of them. But snakes just don't take to me like they do to some of them other boys, so Big John lets me sleep in the big house."

The blonde was beginning to look suspicious. "Snakes ten feet long? Is that what they call a Texas tall tale?"

"Oh, no, ma'am," John assured her. "I only lie when Big John tells me to, like when the income tax people ask questions about his trips to Europe and the thirty dependents that he swears are his illegitimate children—youngest girl's twenty, you know...."

The blond woman started to laugh. She kept on until tears were rolling down her cheeks, and her companion was giggling audibly. Madeline let go of her own self-control at last, doubling over with laughter.

"Thank you for the profile, Mr. Durango," the tourist laughed at John, her eyes twinkling. "Next time I read a story about you in some magazine, I'll be one of the privileged few who know what a scalawag you really are. Making your men rent their horses...!"

He chuckled. "I've thought about it sometimes," he swore. He pulled out his wallet and handed her a card. "I can always use a good attorney," he told her. "If retirement gets too tough, give me a call." He winked at her. "You're too damned young to retire, honey."

Madeline could have kissed him when she saw the older woman's face begin to glow.

"Thank you," came the heartfelt reply. "Now which way *do* I go to get to Houston?"

After the tourists had driven away, John mounted his gelding, waiting for Madeline to follow suit. He lit a cigarette with steady fingers and led the way toward the barn where his prize bulls were quartered like royalty. They had their own air-conditioning as well as a heating system for winter.

"You scalawag, you," Madeline muttered, trying to tease him out of his black mood.

He didn't even spare her a glance. He was still furious, and she didn't know how she was going to explain her own actions. How could she, when she didn't understand them herself?

"John, what was your father like?" she asked suddenly.

He glanced at her as they rode along. "What brought that on?"

She shrugged. "I don't know. You've never talked about him. I just . . . wondered."

He took a draw on the cigarette and stared at the horizon. "He was rigid. Hard. Very disciplined and single-minded. He had nothing as a child, and he was determined to show the whole damned world that he was as capable of getting rich as anybody else. He was a career man in the Marines before he bought Big Sabine and started drilling for oil.'' He laughed mirthlessly. "What he found didn't amount to much at first, but we invested carefully, bought more land, and got lucky.''

"Your mother?" she asked carefully.

"She died when I was born.''

"Oh.'' Madeline stared at the red coats of the bulls as they neared the barn. "The ranch was named for a battle, wasn't it?" she murmured.

"The battle of Sabine Pass,'' he agreed, "where my father was born. In 1863, Union troops tried to invade Texas through the pass. Two lieutenants named Richard Dowling and N.H. Smith defended the fort there with six cannon and forty-two men. That defense was so successful that Union troops never tried to invade through the pass again.''

"I'll bet your father liked the odds when he heard the story, didn't he?" she asked with a tiny smile.

"Impossible odds?" he mused. "Yes. That appealed to him, all right. The only thing that didn't was fatherhood. He spent the first twenty years of my life blaming me for my mother's death. It was just as well that he left me with my uncle while he was in the service.''

She studied his rigid profile wonderingly. She was curious about him in new ways; she wanted to know what forces had shaped him into the man he was.

He dismounted at the fence and hooked his boot on the lowest rung, leaning his arms over it to watch a huge Santa Gertrudis bull lumber along in his solitary pasture.

Madeline joined him by the fence, drawn by his strength and size, as she thought about the lonely young boy he must have been. She liked the closeness—perhaps, she told herself, because of the faint chill in the air. John radiated warmth at this range. Her eyes swept over him—from the long, powerful legs up to the broad leather belt around his lean waist, the massive chest and muscular arms. His forearms were dark with the same sprinkling of hair that covered the rest of his body, and there was a thin gold watch strapped over his wrist. He wore no rings at all and had beautiful hands—broad, tanned, with long fingers and a feathering of hair over their backs. The nails were flat, neatly trimmed and immaculate, despite the manual labor he did when at the ranch.

"Are you considering taking up art?" he asked with a lash in his voice. "You must have me memorized by now."

She dragged her eyes back to the bull. "I was thinking," she said shortly. "You just sort of got in the way."

"Thinking about what?" he prodded. "Your next murder victim?"

It was the first sign of melting in the glacier he'd drawn around himself, and she met his look with a shy smile.

"Not quite," she assured him. "Only the vile tools I'm going to need and the grisly details."

He laughed softly, bending his head to light a cigarette. "Who's going to get the ax this time?" he asked.

She peeked up at him. "I thought I'd kill off the detective-hero."

"Your fans would hang you from the nearest tree," he commented. He glanced down at her, his eyes taking in the long, waving disarray of her red gold hair in the early-morning light, the flush of her cheeks, the sparkle in her green eyes. They narrowed. "A more unlikely murderess..." he murmured.

She smiled pertly. "I've always loved detective fiction," she said with a sigh. "Solving crimes. I wanted to be a policewoman, but I was too busy covering news."

"Ever miss it?" he asked with genuine curiosity.

"Reporting, you mean?" She thought back to those days. It seemed so long ago, when she was sole reporter and photographer for a small-town weekly newspaper. "I'm not sure. Sometimes I think I'd give anything to go back to it. It was so uncomplicated, compared to what I do now, so cut and dried. I didn't have to create the news, only report it."

"I shouldn't think it was so hard finding new ways to kill people," he said with a teasing glance.

She laughed. "You'd be surprised. Competition is fierce, you know, and I'm the new kid on the block. I've got to be the best I can be, or I'll go on unemployment in no time."

"I liked *The Grinding Tower*," he remarked.

"Thank you."

He grinned. "The hero had some . . . familiar characteristics."

She felt herself flushing as she recalled her detective: tall, broad-shouldered, with a mustache, a taste for Scotch whiskey and a habit of forcing his equipment to go more than the last mile. Yes, she'd patterned him after John, but she hadn't expected . . .

"Want to sue me?" she asked with a shy glance.

"I'm too flattered to sue you." He tilted his hat lower across his eyes. They narrowed, running down the length of her body and back up again. "The heroine sounded a little like you," he remarked.

She met his eyes and felt her pulse leap wildly. She hadn't realized that. "Did she?" she murmured.

The dark, intent look on his face made her nervous. "Why did you run away from me, just before those tourists showed up? Was it what I said about being without sleep? Did you think I'd spend the night with Melody?"

Her breath caught in her throat. How well he read her! She swallowed. "I . . . I just wanted to ride a little faster, that's all."

"Was it?" He reached out, tucking a careless finger into the V-neck of her blouse to tug her gently toward him. But he didn't release his hold on her. That long, maddening finger slowly traced the beginning slope of her breasts under the thin fabric. She was suddenly and shyly aware that she wasn't wearing a bra. And judging by the look on his dark, taut face, he'd just discovered that as well.

The effect of the light, disturbing caress was beginning to be very visible, especially to the silver eyes that dropped pointedly to the thrust of her high, small breasts against the thin cotton.

His eyes moved back up to capture hers, to watch the nervous excitement sparkle in them. She tried to back away from that tantalizing finger, but he slid a rough hand around to her back and caught her, forcing her slender body against the long, powerful lines of his own.

"Oh, no, you don't, honey," he murmured, and his hand spread out at her throat, so big that it almost covered the tops of her breasts in a contact that wasn't really intimate but had the full effect of intimacy.

"John, what are you doing?" she squeaked, her fingers clutching at his big arms to push him away.

"What do you think I'm doing?" he growled. "I'm making a pass at you. What does it feel like?"

She gaped up at him, fascinated, frightened, her body trembling as if he'd stripped her and was stroking her naked skin. "You've never touched me . . ." she whispered.

"You've never wanted me to," he reminded her. His hands slid down her body to her buttocks, pressing her hips into his in an intimacy that she should have protested, but didn't— couldn't. "Until last night."

"I didn't," she protested weakly.

"You were so jealous of Melody, you could hardly see straight," he accused tautly. His hands pressed her closer to his blatant masculinity. "As if you had a damned thing to be jealous of . . . come here!"

Even as he spoke he bent his head and for the first time she felt the hard, warm crush of his mouth over hers. The mustache tickled and his lips were roughly insistent, forcing her mouth to open, to admit the sharp, deep penetration of his tongue. She felt it teasing hers as his hands moved up, sliding under the blouse to caress the softness of her bare back.

She gasped and a long, shuddering moan slipped from her throat as her fingernails involuntarily dug into his big arms. He smelled of smoke and saddle leather and expensive cologne, and his big body was damp where she was riveted to it. It was incredible, to be making love in broad daylight, to be kissed so passionately, held so intimately, by John....

"Kiss me back," he ground out against her trembling lips. "You wanted to touch me earlier, do it now. Stop holding back, damn it!"

The words were like a dash of cold water, penetrating the fiery mist of passion. She looked up into a face hard with passion, into silvery eyes that glittered with new, barely leashed hunger.

She shook her head as if to clear it. "No," she whispered, disbelieving. Her mouth hurt from the hungry pressure of his, her knees felt like rubber. "No, we're... just friends...."

He took her hand and pressed it, palm flat against the furious shudder of his heart, breathing heavily as he watched her face. "Feel what you do to me," he growled, "what you've always done to me. Just friends? Like sweet hell, we are!"

"No!" She dragged herself out of his arms, her eyes as wild as her hair as she moved out of his reach and stood trying to catch her breath. "I won't let it happen, I won't!"

"It already has," he said curtly. His eyes slid over her rigid body, up over the pointed tautness of her breasts, taking in the accelerated breath-

ing that caused her chest to rise and fall un-
evenly.

With a cry of mingled shock and outrage, she
turned and ran for her horse. This wasn't happening, it couldn't be, not with John; not with the
only man she trusted. What he was offering was
too sudden, too unexpected.

"Madeline!" he shot at her.

She was already astride the little mare, her eyes
wild as she looked at him.

"It's too late to run from it," he said quietly,
his gaze dark and steady.

"Oh, no, it isn't," she said in a choked voice.
"I won't see you again, John."

"You will," he said softly. "Because what we
just had wasn't enough—for either of us."

With a muffled curse, she whirled the mare and
urged her quickly into a gallop, the wind tearing
through her hair. Never, she thought wildly,
never, John Durango! She closed her eyes against
the memory of his hard, expert mouth, against
remembered pleasure. The horrible thing was that
he was right, it hadn't been enough....

Chapter Four

Madeline walked around in a daze for the rest of the morning, wondering at the lightning change in her relationship with John. She was confused by her own reaction to him, by the vague hungers he'd created. She thought she was frigid after her brief, disastrous relationship with Allen. She'd thought she was immune.

Allen. She hadn't thought about him in a long time, but the hurt came back with diminished force as she sat over her electric typewriter looking at the splatters of rain that started to fall against the windowpanes.

It had happened over two years ago. She'd met Allen at a writer's club meeting. He was an architect who dreamed of writing a novel and

Madeline had encouraged him. He hadn't sold his book idea—sadly, he didn't have the talent to back up his ambition. But while Madeline had been trying to help him, she'd also been falling in love. And *he'd* encouraged *her,* promising happiness, promising forever. His ardor had been demanding, persistent. In the end, he'd worn her down.

The morning after she'd given in to him, she woke up with memories of more discomfort than pleasure but dreams of happier nights together. And then he'd dropped the bomb. He'd begun to tell her about his wife, about how trapped he was. There was a little boy. He begged her to forgive him, he must have been out of his mind, but he'd wanted her so much and he'd had no idea that she was a virgin....

She got up from the typewriter and walked aimlessly around the room. The memory of that day was the blackest in her life. She'd almost gone over the deep edge. She could remember being very calm about it, ushering Allen to the door, closing it quietly behind him without a word. She'd made herself a pot of coffee and had gone to the typewriter to work with a fury all the rest of the day. Then she'd had a few drinks and decided to go for a walk in the rain—in the middle of the night. She wound up at the opera, which was miles away, and couldn't even remember how she'd gotten there. But she started across the street in the driving downpour. And suddenly there had been the scream of brakes. A tall, furiously angry man in dark evening clothes and a white dress Stetson had climbed out of the white Rolls Royce and proceeded to give her hell.

That had been her introduction to John Cameron Durango, who'd paused in the middle of his furious tirade to lift her gently into the front seat of the elegant car. He'd taken her home with him to the penthouse apartment where he stayed when he couldn't get out to the ranch. John had given her dry clothes, plied her with good black coffee, walked her until her legs ached and put her to bed in his guest room. It was the beginning of a strange and beautiful friendship, and the instant rapport they'd established that night had never diminished. They'd found worlds of things they had in common, and had finally reached a point where he could start a sentence and she'd finish it. He seemed to actually read her mind.

She went over last night and this morning again and again, wondering at her own odd behavior at the party. She had been jealous of that little blonde, and because of it she'd flirted harder than usual with John.

Over the years she'd been curious about him more than once; she'd wondered how it would feel to be kissed by him. Now she knew. Oh, how she knew!

Her own hungers shocked her. She'd promised herself that she'd never let another man get as close as Allen had, that she'd never let herself be hurt again. But she knew she was never going to be able to keep John Durango at arm's length. He was as bullheaded as she was, and years more experienced—thirty-nine to her twenty-seven. He, too, had loved and lost, though Madeline hadn't known him when his wife Ellen died. Since then he'd been seen with a trail of women, except for the past year or so.

He'd been extremely selective recently, as if his playboy image had begun to bother him. The gossips had gone wild over that about-face, wondering if there was a special woman in his life. But John's private life was exactly that, private, and he shared it with no one except Madeline. And there was a lot that he kept even from her. She'd been curious about his affairs with women, curious about his marriage, but she'd never asked.

She wasn't sure she would have liked the answers.

The phone rang suddenly, and she jumped. She ran to answer it, vaguely hoping that it might be John. Was he going to pursue her so quickly?

She grabbed the receiver with trembling hands, her heart slamming wildly in her chest as all kinds of pictures flashed across her mind.

"Hello?" she whispered.

A chuckle came over the line—a voice not as deep as John's—and Madeline's heart sank. "My goodness, who were you expecting?" Donald Durango laughed. "I'll have to tell Cousin John that he's got competition."

"Oh, hi, Donald," Madeline said, recovering quickly. "How are you this morning?"

"Just fine. You left so suddenly last night, I never got a chance to issue my invitation to supper tonight," Donald said. "How about it? I'll have Maisie fix pepper steak and peach cobbler," he added temptingly.

She glanced out the window at the rain which was now streaming down the windowpanes and frowned. "I don't know. It looks pretty awful outside, and they're predicting heavy thunderstorms...."

"Are you sure that's the reason?" Donald teased. "It wouldn't have anything to do with the fact that Big John would explode if he knew you were spending the evening with me?"

"Don't be silly," she chided. "I'm not afraid of John, and he doesn't tell me with whom I can associate."

"He'd like to, especially where I'm concerned," he reminded her.

"John has a blind spot about you," she told him with a laugh. "He just doesn't appreciate your great intelligence and charm the way I do, though heaven knows I've tried to help him."

Donald sighed. "It's my own fault in a way. If I hadn't been with Ellen so much... He hasn't been the same since she died. Well, how about supper?" he asked gruffly.

That bit about Ellen hurt unexpectedly. Of course John had loved his wife, they'd been childhood sweethearts, and the wedding had had a Cinderella quality about it. Madeline had read about John Durango years before she met him. He was a legend in Texas politics as well as business.

"Supper?" she murmured absently. "Well, I suppose I could."

"I'll come after you," he assured her. "About five-thirty?"

"That sounds fine. See you." She hung up, staring at the receiver.

It wasn't going to please John that she was having a meal with his cousin, but then, she'd never knuckled under like most women he knew. She lived her own life in her own way.

She stared at the typewriter keys blankly. It still seemed like a dream. Her whole body tingled with the memory of John's hungry ardor, the feel of his hands touching her.

"Go away, John, and let me work!" she muttered aloud. Even when he was out of sight, he haunted her. Was this what she could expect from now on?

The skies were dark and the rain was violent, when Donald came by for her.

"I'm glad you came after me," Madeline told the blond-headed man at the wheel of the big Lincoln.

Donald tossed a blue-eyed glance in her direction and grinned boyishly. "No doubt. It's not the best time to drive around for fun."

She leaned back against the seat, and the action made her slinky black pantsuit cling even closer to her slender body. She sighed. "Funny, you driving a Lincoln," she murmured, "and John driving a Ferrari. Personality-wise, it's odd. You really ought to switch cars."

"John only looks conservative, darling," he chuckled. "I *am* conservative. The cars match us exactly. It's just that you don't know Cousin John quite as well as you think."

"What an understatement," she murmured, remembering his kiss with a vividness that destroyed her peace of mind.

"Your trouble, little lady," he said conversationally, "is that you're repressed. What you need is a man."

She blinked at him. "Stuffed or mounted?" she asked politely.

He laughed delightedly, guiding the big car around a deep puddle of water in the middle of the lane. "Writers," he murmured.

"Artists," she murmured back with a laughing, sideways glance. "What are you doing these days?"

"Getting ready for an exhibit, as usual," he informed her. "Which is why I wanted you over for supper—you can help me pick the twenty best canvases. I've already brought my favorites down from the garage apartment where I usually work and arranged them all around the living room for your inspection.''

''I'm flattered.''

He glanced at her. ''You ought to be. I'm particular about letting people see my work before it's on display.''

She smiled. ''I've never understood why you work so hard at painting. Granted, you're very talented; but you're filthy rich.''

''I scratch where it itches,'' he replied nonchalantly. ''And it makes John mad as hell when I exhibit in the bank where *he's* a major stockholder,'' he added with a grin.

''You aren't!'' she burst out.

He tossed her a triumphant smile. ''Oh, yes, indeed.''

Madeline laughed in spite of herself. She could see John turning the air blue. It wasn't so much that he disliked art as that he disliked being put in a position where he had to be courteous to his hated cousin. Even the head of Durango Oil couldn't raise hell in the lobby of a very conservative bank—it wouldn't be good for business. And it might give the edge to the competition— where Donald was the major stockholder.

''You and John are worse than the business rivals in that TV series we all watch and love,'' she accused him. "Are you sure you haven't been taking lessons?"

He scratched his blond head. "Now that you mention it, I did just happen to jot down a note or two."

She leaned back with a sigh. "Looks like I may have to take one or two of my own—from that nice lady who always separates the bad guys."

"You do that, sugar," he teased. "But don't stand in the middle."

"Never," she promised. Her eyes followed a thin streak of lightning down to the horizon. "Whew, it's getting rough out here!" she said. "The last time we had electrical storms like this, we had a tornado or two."

"Never happen," he assured her. "It's just a little lightning. Relax."

He turned the corner and pulled the car in between the two stone pillars that marked the long driveway to his suburban house. Parking the car up in front of the sprawling brick house, he cut the engine. "Want me to fetch you an umbrella, or will you risk that elaborate hairdo under your cute little hat?"

She touched the brim of the beige rain hat that matched her coat and smiled. "I'll make a mad dash for the door, if you don't mind. I tend to trip over umbrellas and have them open unexpectedly in cars."

"Suit yourself. Here goes!"

Dinner was delicious. Maisie, plump and petite, hovered over them—setting food on the table, refilling coffee cups, taking away empty dishes—so unobtrusively that she didn't interrupt the lazy flow of conversation.

Afterward, Madeline followed Donald around the living room, frowning over the delightful landscapes that were his specialty. With their delicate pastels and misty settings, they had a fairyland quality, an elusiveness that was unique. Madeline had one of Donald's paintings herself. It occupied a place of honor over her mantel, and when she was particularly troubled she sometimes felt as if she could walk into the tranquil scene.

"Odd," she murmured, studying a painting of a gazebo in a rose garden, "how tranquil your paintings are, when you aren't tranquil at all."

"We all need bits of peace at times," he murmured.

She lifted the canvas. "Definitely this one, and . . . oh!"

She jumped at the sudden flash that was immediately followed by darkness and a thunderclap that shook the whole house. She almost dropped the painting from the shock. The room was pitch-black.

"What happened?" she gasped.

"Power lines are down somewhere," he muttered. There were odd noises, like canvases falling, easels being displaced, chairs being knocked over, accompanied by muffled curses. "I've got a flashlight around here somewhere. Aha, here it is! I'll just turn it on and...damn!" There was a rattling, a metallic sound. "No batteries," he sighed, and there was a thud.

"How about a candle?" she suggested.

"Oh, I've got two of those, right here beside me."

"Well, light one!" she called. She wrapped her arms around herself, feeling chilled and a little frightened in the darkness.

"With what?" he asked politely.

"A match, stupid!"

"I don't smoke!" he shot back.

"Then rub two of your easels together and make a fire," she grumbled. "Be resourceful!"

"Come over here and kiss me," he said with a gleeful theatrical laugh, "and we'll set the place aflame!"

She laughed defeatedly. "Well, then ... ah!" The lights came back on and she slumped with relief.

"Fast work," Donald muttered, rubbing his knee.

"I hate Houston in the spring," she said, leaning against the table for a minute. "The humidity and the rain are bad enough, but the thunderstorms are truly awful."

"Amen. Now, back to the job at hand, my dear...."

A week went by, a slow miserable week during which she made a stab at beginning the research on her latest book and set up an appointment with a friend in the police department, to learn something more about murder, drugs and drug dealing.

But all the while, her rebellious mind was on John and the feel of his arms crushing her against his powerful body, and the taste of his hard mouth on hers. She walked around aching, wondering how it would have been if she'd opened his shirt and touched him the way she'd wanted to, if she'd given in completely and kissed him back. She still didn't understand what was happening to her, but it was slowly sapping her strength, her pride, her willpower.

Friday rolled around and she glared at the telephone on her desk, hating it because it hadn't rung. Perhaps John was out of town. Or, worse, perhaps he didn't plan to call her. She'd said she didn't want to see him again. Surely he hadn't taken her seriously?

She chewed on her lower lip, her eyes riveted to the phone. After a minute, she picked up the receiver and began to dial John's number, hating her own weakness. But she had to find out if they were on speaking terms.

Josito answered. "Why, hello, *señorita*," he said, his voice surprised.

"Hello, Josito. Uh, is John around?"

"Sí," he said, still uncertain.

"He, uh, hasn't been out of town or anything?"

"No, *señorita*, , he is here at the ranch. Surely he has phoned you?"

"No," she grumbled, "he hasn't. Where is he?"

He laughed amusedly. "You will not believe it."

"That bad, huh? Where is he? Come on, Josito, if you tell me, I'll tell you who's going to get the knife in the sequel to *The Grinding Tower*," she added temptingly, knowing the diminutive man's passion for her work.

"You will?" She could almost see his face lighting up. He laughed. "All right, then. He is helping the men hay the Johnson bottoms."

"John?" she burst out. "But he hates haying—he'd rather dig post holes." She frowned. "Why is he helping? With that baler-loader of his, all it takes is a couple of men."

"The machine, it is not working," came the amused reply.

She sighed. "Again, huh? I'll bet the mechanics have run out of words to call it by now. Well, what is he doing, rolling it into big round bales?"

Josito sighed. "He is doing it the old way, as usual," he said.

"This I've got to see. The Johnson bottoms?"

"*Sí, señorita.* And now," he said sternly, "who gets the knife?"

"Raggins," she replied, laughing at his intake of breath. "Well, the old devil deserves it, don't you think?"

"Oh, *sí!* Most definitely!"

"I hate the silly man, too," she admitted. "Imagine enjoying a murder. There's something wrong with a world that makes entertainment out of tragedy, don't you think?"

"That is for the philosophers, *señorita*." Josito laughed. "Not for me."

"Well, I'm going to see John. Uh, he isn't in a bad mood or anything?" she fished.

"Black," he said. "Absolutely black, *señorita*. One hopes that his mood will improve someday. It is discouraging to spend hours creating the perfect soufflé, only to have it flung into the soup because it was creased."

"He didn't!"

"*Sí*. That was just before he poured the coffee into the rubber tree plant because it was too weak."

"Oh, the poor rubber tree," she moaned.

"Poor me," he corrected. "Señorita Vigny, if you need a victim for your next book..." he suggested hopefully.

"You wouldn't want me to knock off my friend, would you?" she teased.

"He is nobody's friend in this mood," he muttered. "Business must be indeed wearing to make him so unpleasant."

"I'll see if I can cheer him up for you," she promised, more nervous than ever. "Thanks, Josito."

She stopped by a package store on the way and got a twelve-pack of beer. It was blazing hot, almost summer, and the sun was high. Presumably John wouldn't be alone, and if she remembered the old-fashioned way of haying, they'd all appreciate something cool to drink. After the hay baler made neat work of the yellow green hay, it was left in long rows in the field. A platform truck would drive along between the rows, the men walking alongside heaving the bales up onto the slow-moving truck. It was a long, arduous process, much harder than haying with a unit that baled and stacked all in one. Of course, John had one of those units. But it was ten years old and ready to junk, and he wouldn't replace it because the mechanics could still fix it.

When she got to the Johnson bottoms, near the river, there were two men attacking the broken-down machine with tools, red faced and cursing, while John and half the ranch hands walked alongside two huge platform trucks and tossed bales onto them. There were storm clouds looming on the horizon, and Madeline suddenly understood why so many workers had been turned loose on this one field. The hay had to be in before the rain.

Madeline parked the little yellow Volkswagen at the beginning of a row and cut the engine, counting heads. There would be just enough beer to go around.

It took John a minute to see her, but when he did, he made a beeline in her direction. He was bare to the waist, his hair-matted chest and flat stomach like polished bronze, slick with sweat; his battered black hat jammed down over his eyes. He was peeling off the thick work gloves as he came, his face as dark as the storm clouds gathering in the distance.

He opened the passenger door and eased his jean-clad legs inside the small car. The scent of hay and pure man filled the car as he turned, an arm over the back of the seat, to stare at her.

"Hi," she said nervously, shy with him as she'd never been before.

"Hi, yourself," he said curtly. "What are you doing here?"

She stared into his hard face, remembering vividly the feel of his mouth on hers, the brush of the mustache on her sensitive skin, the blaze of desire in his silver eyes.

"Uh, research for my next book," she said, indicating the cans of beer. "Poisoned beer. I'm looking for volunteers so I can see the grisly effects."

The mustache twitched involuntarily, and he studied her smiling face as if he hadn't seen it for years.

"I think I can find you a couple," he murmured. He drew in a deep, slow breath and removed the hat, wiping his forearm over his brow. "God, it's hot out there."

"Don't you want a beer?" she asked, reaching for a frosty tall can.

He caught her wrist gently, and the smile faded as he looked straight into her eyes.

"No, I don't want a beer," he said softly. "Not just yet. You don't like the taste of it, do you?"

She shook her head, feeling oddly breathless at the growing darkness in his eyes.

He dropped his hat onto the floorboard and leaned toward her, his eyes lowering to her full, parted lips. "I'm going to kiss you first," he breathed, his hand going to her throat to ease her head back against the seat as he bent closer. "It's all I've thought about for days!"

Her fingers went up to tangle in the thick hair at the nape of his neck, drawing him near, her eyes on his hard, sensuous mouth. "I was afraid . . . you'd be angry," she whispered shakily.

"Don't talk. Open your mouth for me," he said huskily, his lips parting to take hers.

She felt the kiss like a volt of electricity shattering her body. She gasped involuntarily, clinging to him, her half-opened eyes looking straight into his.

"My God, you wanted it as much as I did, didn't you?" he whispered gruffly.

He crushed her mouth under his, his tongue darting possessively into her mouth, his body pressing hers back against the seat. She moaned at the hunger he was creating, feeling the abrasive softness of the mustache as his mouth moved with expert sureness against hers. His tongue traced the inner softness of her lips, easing past her teeth to move slowly, suggestively, inside her mouth until she moaned sharply.

His fingers trailed down from her throat to her breasts, outlined by the yellow sundress she was wearing. He traced its low neckline with a caressing touch that caused her fingernails to bite into him.

His mouth bit at hers softly, brushing, teasing. His knuckles skimmed maddeningly over the soft skin left bare by the dipping neckline, barely touching, tormenting her until she arched toward them involuntarily with a faint cry that was muffled under his hungry mouth.

"I can't touch you like this," he whispered against her bruised lips, "in front of half my cowboys. Is that what you want, Satin, to feel my hands on you under the dress, against your bare skin?"

"John . . . !" she cried out, burying her face in his throat while tears dampened her eyes from the intense emotion he'd aroused. Her hands moved down to his chest, helplessly touching him, savoring the hair-roughened feel of his skin under her fingers, the strength in the hard muscles.

His big arms swallowed her, holding her hard and close while she clung to him, trying desperately to get her own shattered emotions back under control. She felt an ache that seemed to go all the way to her soul, an unfamiliar ache that she barely understood.

"I shouldn't have done that," he whispered in her ear. "We were both too hungry for it."

She drew back a little, her eyes wet with tears as they searched his. "I feel strange," she whispered.

"So do I," he said quietly. "I hurt in a way I haven't since I was fifteen. You weren't the only one who caught fire."

She stared into the fiery gray depths of his eyes helplessly. "I missed you," she said without meaning to.

"I know. I missed you, too." He brushed the unruly hair away from her cheeks with a tender hand. "I thought I'd frightened you away for good, and I didn't know what in hell to do about it."

She reached up to touch his mouth, the hard curve of his chiseled lips under the smooth, furry mustache. It was exciting to be able to touch him, without having him push her away or get angry.

"I'll shave it off, if you want me to," he said against her fingers.

She shook her head, smiling. "I like it." The smile became mischievous. "In fact, I think I might get one for myself. A handlebar mustache... I could wear it on special occasions."

"Not around me," he said firmly. "I don't much like you in trousers, Satin."

"You old-fashioned male chauvinist pig," she said in her haughtiest tone, teasing him and loving every second of it. All the brittle tension between them seemed to have melted away in that one, hungry kiss.

"You've got gorgeous legs," he continued, unabashed, his eyes traveling down the skirt of the dress to her bare calves.

"So have you," she said with a grin.

He chuckled. "Remember that from sponging me down, do you?"

She laughed up at him. "Hairy, but gorgeous," she amended. "No, really, most men don't have nice legs. They have pale, skinny ones. Yours are nice and tan and masculine."

He smiled at her. "What an admission," he murmured with a twinkle in his silver eyes. "I didn't think you'd ever noticed that I had a body."

"It's very hard to miss," she observed dryly.

He caught a strand of her loosened hair and tugged at it, bringing her face close to his. Her eyes were wide and dreamy, her mouth slightly swollen from the long, sweet pressure of his.

"Kiss me," he murmured, bending. His mouth brushed hers and she looped her arms around his neck, her eyes closing as she felt his mouth crush against hers lazily, easily, as if he had all day. It wasn't a threatening pressure at all, nothing to frighten her; just a warm, rough kiss.

He drew back with a faint smile. "How about the ballet tonight?" he asked. "I've got tickets for *Swan Lake.*"

Her face lit up. "I'd love to!"

"I'll pick you up about six. We'll have a late supper at my apartment. I'll have Josito go over and get it started before I come by for you."

She nodded, searching his face. "You're different, like this," she said.

He drew in a long, slow breath as he returned that intent look. "So are you, honey. Sweeter than I dreamed...."

She lowered her eyes. "Go drink your poisoned beer and bale your hay. Poor old tired thing," she murmured, eyeing the broken-down machine with the two cursing mechanics grumbling over it. "If you had any compassion in you, you'd give it a decent burial and buy a new one."

"Not," he told her, "until it gives out completely. I'm not replacing a perfectly good machine."

"It's ten years old!"

"I've got a horse ten years old, and he works better now than he ever did."

"He's probably terrified that you'll turn those mechanics loose on him," she returned.

He leaned forward and kissed her mouth, hard. "See you later."

He opened the door and got out, beer in hand. She stared at his broad back as he moved away, holding up the frosty cans to the obvious delight of his co-workers. Madeline started the little car and drove away, thankful that she was driving, not walking. Her knees didn't feel too strong at the moment.

Chapter Five

Swan Lake had never been lovelier. The ballerinas looked like fairies as they floated through the sensuous ballet. Of course, the fact that John caught her hand at the beginning and held it warmly and tightly until intermission had nothing to do with her exhilaration.

He smoked his cigarette silently during intermission, his turbulent eyes never leaving Madeline. In her long, silky gold dress, she was a sight to hold any man's eyes.

"I like you in that color," he said quietly. "It brings out those tiny gold flecks in your eyes."

She smiled. "You don't look bad yourself," she returned, letting her eyes run down the dark elegance of his evening clothes. "There's a brunette a row over from us who hasn't paid any attention at all to the dancers. She's been too busy leering at you."

"Oh?" A corner of his mustache was raised in a wicked smile. "You'll have to point her out to me, won't you?"

"Not on your life," she said with a surge of pure jealousy. She frowned and turned away. "Hadn't we better go back in?"

He moved in front of her, catching her under the chin to raise her confused eyes to his.

"Be possessive," he said curtly. "I like it."

She caught her breath at the emotion in his deep voice, the look in his glittering eyes.

"I don't have any hold on you, John," she said steadily. "Remember, you told me once that you didn't like people getting too close."

"People, not you," he returned. "My God, come as close as you like. I won't push you away."

"You've been doing it for weeks," she said, searching his eyes.

A muscle tightened in his jaw. "Don't you know why?" he asked with a bitter laugh. "Haven't you figured it out yet?"

Remembering the way he'd kissed her, the way he'd looked at her, touched her, she was beginning to understand a lot more about his recent behavior.

She looked away, faintly embarrassed by that wild flare of passion they'd shared in the fields. Their relationship had changed so subtly she'd hardly been aware of it. She couldn't even think of him in platonic terms anymore. She'd wanted his mouth with a kind of violence, she'd wanted his hands on her bare skin, his eyes devouring her....

She was barely aware of people moving past them, the buzz of conversation drifting away as the audience filed through the doors into the auditorium. Her eyes were locked with John's all of a sudden, and she felt frozen to the spot.

The smoking cigarette, forgotten in his fingers, sent curls of gray smoke up toward the ceiling.

"That's right, look at me," he said huskily, watching the curious intensity of her green eyes as they traveled over his hard face.

"You're ... very pleasant to look at," she said involuntarily.

"That's not what I meant," he said curtly. His chest rose and fell heavily. "You're just beginning to see me as a man, aren't you?"

The conversation was beginning to disturb her. She fumbled with her purse, avoiding his eyes. "I always have," she murmured.

"Not exactly. Not in the way you've noticed me for the past few weeks." He lifted the cigarette to his chiseled mouth with a faint smile. "What's behind this sudden compulsion you seem to have about touching me?"

Her eyes spit green fire at him. "I'm a physical person," she muttered.

"Like hell," he replied pleasantly. "You never touch anybody, honey, male or female. That was one of the first things I noticed about you when we met. You're fastidious in that sense."

"I never knew my mother," she reminded him. "And my father wasn't outwardly affectionate, even though we were close."

"I wasn't asking for an explanation, I was simply wondering why you like to touch me," he continued.

She clutched the purse tightly. Perhaps if she got a running start . . .

"Oh, hell, why do I start these conversations?" he asked the ceiling. "Do you want to watch the ballet or go see if Josito's got supper ready?" His mustache twitched. "That beer you brought me didn't last long. And it's the only thing I've put in my stomach all day.''

"John!" she gasped, forgetting her irritation with him. "No breakfast?"

"Wasn't time," he replied. "The damned machine broke down and it looked like rain. When we finally got through, I rushed home to shower and shave and dress for the ballet."

"Why didn't you say so?" she chided. "I wouldn't have minded missing the ballet, truly I wouldn't. Let's go, before you pass out from hunger and I have to drag you out of here by your pants' legs."

"That might cause some interesting speculations," he murmured.

She laughed up at him, once more on familiar footing. "With my luck, someone who reads my books would see us and think I was acting out my next plot." She lowered her voice conspiratorially. "Dragging my latest victim off to a secret grave after inflicting a fatal wound with some untraceable instrument."

"Like that icicle you used in *The Grinding Tower?*" he asked with a chuckle.

"It was a big icicle," she reminded him. She grinned devilishly. "And impossible to trace, except for the huge patch of wetness on the victim's shirt, remember?''

"Which your dauntless detective, Matt McDuncan, spotted at the onset. When he found a water spot on the suspect's jacket sleeve, he knew immediately who the perpetrator was!''

She laughed delightedly. "I was afraid that was going to be terribly obvious, but the readers swallowed it.''

"Fans are always loyal," he reminded her. His eyes narrowed. "I even forgave you for that rotten crack about McDuncan using the typewriter even with five keys missing because 'he never used those particular letters, anyway.'''

She followed him out to the Ferrari, hurrying as a few large raindrops spattered down, and let him put her in the passenger seat, still laughing. "Sorry about that," she murmured. "But John, you do push equipment to the absolute limit.''

He got in beside her, started the big engine, and pulled out into traffic with the smooth motions of an old race car driver—a sport which John had dabbled in years ago.

"Old habits die hard, honey," he reminded her. "When I went to live with my father and we started drilling for oil, we had to jury rig equipment to keep going financially. We could hold a car together with baling wire and hairpins."

"And now you can afford a Ferrari and a Rolls," she smiled. "And I'll bet part of you misses those old days."

He lit a cigarette. "Most of me misses them," he admitted. He leaned back against the seat, weaving in and out of traffic lazily. "I used to have time to go riding early in the mornings every day—the way we did last week," he added, glancing at her quietly.

She stared out at the night lights of Houston glowing through the rain-streaked windshield. "And direct misguided tourists to snake-filled bunkhouses?" she said, trying to make a joke of it.

He laughed shortly. "Not exactly. I had her going for a little bit."

"Until you mentioned that part about the ten-foot snakes," she teased. "And the houseful of illegitimate daughters . . ."

"I used to have women running in and out of my house," he admitted, his face thoughtful. "Before I married Ellen."

She shifted restlessly in the seat. "And since?" She didn't like hearing about his wife.

"I'll be forty years old in September, Madeline," he said, his tone strangely subdued, solemn. "The business takes up practically every waking hour, and I have to sleep sometimes. That's what I meant, about missing the old days. I didn't have a lot of money, but I had a lot of time."

"You make yourself sound like Methuselah," she grumbled. Her eyes traced his big body. "My gosh, you could run circles around most of your vice-presidents."

"You've got that backward," he said. "Most of them have kids. They stay active by playing with them."

There was a bitterness in his tone, and she turned in the seat to look at his hard profile. "You want children, don't you?" she asked, faintly shocked at the realization.

"Who am I going to leave Big Sabine and Durango Oil to when I die?" he asked quietly, turning into the parking lot under the building that housed his Houston apartment. "My cousin?" he added with a vicious glare in her direction.

She averted her eyes. "Then all you have to do is get married," she said. The thought made her sick. John, married, with children.

He laughed shortly. "What a novel idea," he said gruffly. "I can have it drawn up into a contract, can't I? *X* number of dollars in exchange for a woman's body and one male child."

"Oh, stop it," she said, torn up inside at the cynicism in his voice. "You make it sound so cold-blooded."

"It would be," he replied as he eased the car into a parking spot and cut the engine. His face, in the dim lights of the parking garage, was harder than ever. "If I'm cynical, it's because life's made me that way." He caught a strand of her loosened red gold hair and tugged at it idly. "I told you once that I didn't mind paying for what I wanted. That's true, within limits. But I'm not paying any woman for a son. Children should be born out of love, not business."

"You old romantic, you," she said with a faint smile.

He frowned at her. "Haven't you ever wanted children?"

She averted her face. That was a question so deeply personal, she almost resented it.

"I'm too old for that," she said coolly.

"At twenty-seven?" he burst out. "My God, women are having babies in their forties!" He scowled.

"It's the commitment, isn't it?" he said speculatively. "You might be able to manage a loose commitment to a man someday, but there's no walking away from a child."

She smiled self-consciously. "You know me pretty well."

"Not as well as I'd like to," he said flatly, his eyes suddenly smoldering. "And not in the sense I want to."

"What sense?" she blurted out before she thought.

But he turned away to get out of the car without answering her.

"Are you really afraid of sex?" he asked as they walked toward the elevator, not looking at her.

The question, coming out of the blue, shocked her. She stared up at him, almost stumbling. "Afraid?" She flexed her shoulders under the cobwebby gold shawl she was wearing over her dress. "I don't know. I only tried it once, you know, and it was a pretty brutal introduction."

"He must have hurt you a lot," he said curtly.

"He didn't know I was a virgin until he was past the point of caring," she said, hating the memory. She drew the shawl closer. "I was madly in love, for the first time in my life. Or thought I was. I'll never be vulnerable again, thanks to Allen. He did that much for me.''

"He did nothing for you," he countered, his eyes blazing. He glared down at her as they entered the elevator and he punched a button with a vicious jab. "Are you planning to live the rest of your life the way you are?"

Her green eyes widened. "Like I am?" she prodded.

"Alone," he said.

She leaned back against the wall as the elevator hummed and began to move. "You're alone," she said.

"Not all the time," he said meaningfully.

She glared at him. "I don't believe in casual affairs," she said shortly. "I could never be promiscuous, or give myself out of a purely physical urge."

"And if it was with someone you cared about, who cared about you?" he asked quietly.

Her eyes searched his. "I don't know."

"What about if it was with me?" he asked in a deep, velvety tone.

She looked at him as if he'd just suggested that they catch a bellhop and barbecue him over a fire in the lobby. The expression on her face brought a reluctant smile to his dark face, and a twinkle to his eyes.

"What...are we having for supper?" she asked evasively, her face almost the shade of the red highlights in her hair.

He laughed softly. "Wait and see."

Josito served them a delicious meal of beef burgundy with a crisp chef's salad and home-made rolls, accompanied by a rich port wine with a cheese flan for dessert. John ate his with obvious relish, while Madeline only picked at hers, looking distractedly out the window where flashes of lightning illuminated the jagged shape of the city skyline. What he'd said in the elevator disturbed her. Despite the hunger she had discovered for him, and his equally obvious hunger for her, she'd never consciously let herself think of John as a lover. Now she was forced to think of him in that role, and her own reaction to the idea surprised her.

Her eyes involuntarily skimmed over his hard face, the mouth that had possessed hers so thoroughly. She could almost picture him in bed, his bronzed skin under her hands, that demanding mouth against every inch of her body, his hands touching her intimately.

"Not hungry?" he asked suddenly, leaning back with his second cup of coffee in his hand.

"Uh, not really, no," she said uneasily.

"You look embarrassed." He cocked his head at her, his eyes narrow, searching. "Was it what I asked you in the elevator—if you'd ever thought about making love with me?"

She dropped the coffee cup. The hot liquid splattered all over the linen tablecloth, drenching the remains of her dessert, her napkin, and spilling into her plate. She gasped and jerked back just in time to save her dress.

"Well, that answers that question," John said with a wicked chuckle. "Josito!" he called.

The little white-coated man came running, assuring Madeline that he could save the tablecloth from being stained, and shooed them off into the living room while he cleaned up.

John was still laughing as he sprawled in his big easy chair and shed his jacket and tie. "My God, what a reaction," he murmured as he opened the top few buttons of his ruffled shirt.

"My hand slipped," she said stubbornly. She kicked off her shoes and curled up on the sofa, glaring across at him.

"Sure." He lit a cigarette and drew up a hassock for his elegantly booted feet.

Madeline stared at the hands folded in her lap. "All right, I wasn't expecting to be propositioned by you."

Both heavy eyebrows went up. "I wasn't aware that I'd propositioned you," he said with that silky note in his voice that spelled trouble.

"What would you call it?" she asked, starting slightly as a clash of thunder reverberated through the room.

"A straight-out, honest question," he replied. He took a deep draw from the cigarette. "I want to know if you've ever thought of me as a lover."

"Why?" she countered.

He leaned over and crushed out the barely touched cigarette with a vicious motion. "Because we can't go back," he said shortly. "I told you that earlier, and I meant it. Now that I've had a taste of you, I'm going to want more." He met her eyes levelly. "That's human nature, honey, and you aren't any more immune to me than I am to you."

"Don't rush me...."

"Rush you, for God's sake!" he growled, getting to his feet to tower over her—big and masculine and sensuous with his shirt half unbuttoned over that bronzed, massive chest. "You've had two years!"

"I won't be added to the Ferrari and the ranch and the oil corporation!" she flung at him.

He sighed angrily. "What makes you think you would be?"

"You're so overwhelming, John," she ground out, avoiding his penetrating gaze. "You... possess things."

"I'd like to possess you, all right," he said in a voice she'd never heard before. "All of you, right down to your dainty little feet."

"Hush!" she whispered, glancing toward the kitchen. "Josito will hear you!"

"Josito won't hear anything over this thunder," he informed her. "But if it bothers you..." He stalked off toward the kitchen. There were muffled voices, a pause, and then John came striding back out with Josito right behind him.

"Good night, *señorita*," the little man told Madeline with a mischievous grin, his jacket over his arm. "I will see you later, Señor Durango," he added before he went out the door, closing it firmly behind him.

"Oh, now look what you've done," Madeline wailed, sitting up straighter. "He'll think you're planning to seduce me!"

"I am," he said matter-of-factly.

"That's what you think!" she returned, searching the floor for her shoes. "I'm going home!"

He caught her by the shoulders as she stood up, and held her just in front of him to study her with quiet, searching eyes.

"I know," he said with a sigh. "I'm going too fast."

She looked up at him, feeling dwarfed without her high heels. His hands on her bare shoulders were warm and strangely comforting.

She laughed suddenly, nervously, and dropped her eyes to the wide expanse of chest visible where his elegant shirt was unbuttoned. Its stark whiteness only emphasized his dark tan.

"I feel like a teenage girl on her first real date," she admitted self-consciously. "And I suppose I'm acting like one. It's been such a long time since I've been this close to any man."

"And what's been happening between us is pretty new," he added with a faint smile.

She glanced up at him with the old sparkle in her green eyes. "I'll bet this is a new twist for you," she said with sudden realization.

He cocked a dark eyebrow. "What is?"

"Having potential conquests try to break down doors getting away from you." She let her hands rest against his warm shirtfront, savoring the smooth feel of it. "I imagine you have to beat them off with sticks most of the time."

"I've found a few hiding under the bed," he chuckled. "But you don't fall into the category of a 'conquest.' Or a one-night stand. Or a casual affair."

She caught his silver eyes and searched them. "Then what am I?"

He drew in a deep, slow breath while his hands tightened, drawing her closer. "Something mighty special, if you must know. I trust you."

She laughed. "I *used* to trust you," she said with a wicked look.

"You liked kissing me," he challenged, looking down at her arrogantly. The mustache curled. "That's why you ran like hell. But you didn't stay away long, did you?"

"No," she admitted. She let her forehead rest against him, and it was like homecoming. "I hate the way it's been between us these past few weeks. The arguing, the remoteness . . . I thought about being without you forever, and I couldn't bear it." Her fingers clutched the fabric of his shirt and her eyes closed. "I had to know if you were mad at me."

"So you came rushing over with a twelve-pack of beer in the middle of the day?"

"Something like that." She sighed, and then smiled amusedly. "When I saw you coming, I wasn't sure whether to give it to you or throw it at you. You looked dangerous."

"I felt dangerous. Ask Josito how I've been this past week."

"I hear the rubber tree's made the endangered species list at your house," she murmured.

"So has Josito, if he's been crying on your shoulder," he informed her.

"Don't pick on him. He's nice."

"So am I, as long as you're around," he said.

She drew back to study his craggy face. "Not always," she murmured, her eyes finding secrets hidden in his.

He touched her mouth with a long, gentle finger and traced its soft red contours, watching it intently. "Men are notoriously not nice when they're aroused," he murmured.

"I wouldn't touch that line with insulated gloves," she informed him. "Do I get a second cup of coffee, or had you planned to carry me off to your cave by the hair of my head?"

He laughed shortly. "I wouldn't pull out a single hair if it cost me one of my prize bulls," he said, reaching to bury his hands in it. "I love the feel of it, the wildflower smell of it."

"Poetry?" she whispered.

His eyes met hers. He was so close that she could see the lines beside them, the thickness of his dark eyelashes. His chest rose and fell quickly, roughly where her hands rested. "The only lines that come to mind are about the Light Brigade—want to hear it? Or would you rather I make it up as I go along?"

The contact with his big, warm body was having its usual devastating effect on her. Her lips parted as she watched his head bend.

"Its . . . like a drug, isn't it?" she whispered as his mouth brushed against hers.

"What is?" he murmured, pressing his lips to her cheeks, her closed eyes, her nose.

"Kissing," she replied. Her fingers brushed against the buttons on his shirt and she wanted suddenly to touch him with a hunger that made her tingle all over.

"Ummmmm," he replied, more interested in learning the contours of her face with his lips than in conversation. He bent suddenly and lifted her clear off the floor, moving toward the sofa with her.

"Go slow with me," she whispered, burying her face in his warm throat. "It's been a very long time."

"For both of us," he said enigmatically. He sat down, holding her across his lap, her cheek against his shoulder. "Would you like it blunt, with no dressing up? I'm half-exhausted. I did more work today than I've done in weeks, and I'm feeling it. And tomorrow morning I've got to be up at six to attend a business conference out of town. A little light lovemaking is all I'm up to— despite the fact that I want you like hell every time I touch you."

She breathed a little easier, but her eyes remained troubled. "Where are we going together?" she asked uncertainly.

He brushed the hair away from her eyes gently, studying her like an exquisite painting. "To a new place," he murmured. "Full of discovery and surprises. Don't be afraid."

"Of you?" She smiled up at him. "You're my friend. I'd do anything for you." The smile faded as she searched his darkening eyes. She reached up to touch his mouth, and the mustache was velvety against her fingertips. "Anything, John."

She could feel the heavy, hard shudder of his heartbeat under her. His eyes were turbulent, his hands suddenly rough as they curled her body into his. Outside, the wind and rain raged unnoticed.

"I can't go back to the way we were before," he said quietly. "You *do* realize that? I won't pressure you into something you don't want, but a platonic relationship is out of the question now."

She toyed with a pearly button on his shirt. "Yes, I know that," she admitted. She let her head slide back against his hard-muscled arm, staring up at him lazily, unblinkingly. Her body felt strange, welcoming, her mind registered a new and urgent hunger. Unconsciously, she stretched like a kitten, the lines of her body fluid as it arched slightly, her breasts lifted to push against the clinging gold fabric of her gown.

"My God, don't do that!" he breathed gruffly, watching her.

"Why?" she chided through half-closed eyes.

"You know why, you little redheaded witch!" he growled as he bent his head, and she felt the sudden, hungry crush of his mouth as it took possession of her parted lips.

She turned in his arms, pressing as close as she could, her arms reaching up to hold him while he fed hungrily on her soft, yielding mouth.

She protested only once, gently, when his teeth nipped painfully against her lower lip in his desperate ardor.

He drew back a whisper, his eyes wild, his breath coming like a track runner's. "I hurt you," he said unsteadily.

"It doesn't matter," she breathed, stretching up to him. "Do it again . . ."

His fingers trailed down her throat as he kissed her again, more carefully this time, deeper, his tongue easing slowly, ardently, into the sweet darkness of her mouth. She tensed as she felt his hard fingers at the neckline of her dress, but they didn't trespass. They only tantalized, tracing the neckline with a lazy, tormenting pressure that made her finally arch toward him with a sharp little moan.

"What's wrong?" he murmured wickedly.

She buried her face in his neck, trembling with the hungers he was raising so effortlessly. "John, please . . ." she whispered shakily.

"Like this, Satin, is this what you want?" he asked sensuously, letting his fingers slide with exquisite tenderness over the high, firm curve of her breasts, covered only by the thin gold material.

She stiffened, trembling at the new intimacy she was allowing. Her nails bit into his shoulders at the intensity of emotion the feathery touch ignited.

"Look at me," he whispered gruffly. "Let me see..."

She raised her eyes to his, and he read with pinpoint accuracy the wild, singeing fever he was creating in her slim body.

"Fireworks," she managed, her voice as unsteady as her breathing.

"Is that how it feels?" he asked quietly. He caught one of her slender hands and laid it against his shirt. "Touch me. I'll let you see what it does to me."

Her fingers fumbled with buttons until she had the shirt open all the way to his leather belt. Her eyes hungrily went over the wide expanse of hard muscle and bronzed, hair-covered skin.

"For God's sake, touch me," he breathed, pressing both her hands against his warm, faintly damp skin.

She looked up, fascinated by the pleasure she read in that hard, craggy face as her long fingers smoothed over his skin, catching in the mat of hair, lingering on the firm muscles. She couldn't remember a time in her life when she'd ever wanted to touch a man this way, or been so curious about the feel of muscle and skin. But John's taut body had a delicious masculinity, the sight as well as the feel and smell of it.

She felt him tremble suddenly, and her eyes registered the surprise she felt.

"Shocked?" he asked unsteadily, pressing her hands closer as he bent and brushed his mouth over her eyes, her nose, the corner of her mouth. "This is what happens to you when I touch you, isn't it?"

"Yes," she managed. "But you're a man..."

"And men aren't supposed to show emotion, is that it?" he asked, drawing back to look at her as she lay in the curve of his arm. "I go absolutely crazy when you put your hands on me," he said quietly. "I can't hide it. You please me in ways I can't describe."

She watched him, her eyes soft and hungry, her body eager, waiting. "I feel that way with you," she admitted shyly.

His eyes darkened, to old silver. "Was it that way with him?" he asked suddenly.

He meant Allen, and the hint of jealousy in his deep voice astounded her. "No," she said. "It wasn't anything like this. I imagined myself in love with him, John, but I was never able to really want him. Perhaps that was why it hurt so...." She turned her face away, before he could see it crumple. "I was such a fool!" she ground out, hitting his broad chest with her fist. "Such a silly, blind fool!"

"Don't," he murmured, wrapping her close. He rocked her, as if she were a frightened, hurt child. "Don't. I'm sorry, I didn't mean to say that. You know I wouldn't hurt you for the world, mentally or physically." He buried his lips in her hair. "I only wish I'd known you then, I wish the first time... had been with me," he finished breathlessly, his arms contracting. "I'd have made it a pleasure beyond bearing."

She nuzzled closer, secure and safe in his hard arms, savoring the tenderness she sensed in him. "You're so good to me, John Durango," she whispered. "I... I care about you, very much."

"I... care about you, too," he said after a minute, the words stilted, as if he wasn't used to using them. And probably he wasn't, she mused silently, since he'd admitted himself that he only wanted one thing from his women, and it wasn't love.

She laughed suddenly, softly. "Is it confession time?" she teased lightly.

He laughed, too. "It sounds that way, doesn't it?"

She let her head fall back on his arm and looked up at him with a lazy smile. "Why don't you kiss me some more," she murmured invitingly.

He drew his finger along her throat, down to the silken curve of her breast, in a slow, tantalizing motion, watching the involuntary reaction of her body to the sensual caress.

"Because," he murmured, "I hate doing things halfway." He looked down at her for a long time, his eyes solemn, his face hard. "We're going to be together someday," he said while his hand touched her in a new, exciting way and his eyes watched her helpless reaction. "Totally together, you understand? We arouse each other too much for it not to happen eventually."

"Not . . . yet," she pleaded unsteadily.

"Not yet, honey," he said gently. "Not tonight, especially when I'm dead on my feet and I've got a seven o'clock flight to catch in the morning. But someday."

She searched his silvery eyes in the silence that seemed to stretch between them. "And then, what?" she asked nervously.

"Why don't we let the future take care of itself?" he asked.

She leaned against him. "I don't want to lose you again," she said softly.

"You're never going to," he said curtly, and all at once she found herself flat on her back on the couch with his arms on either side of her head. "I won't let that happen, Madeline."

Her breath came hard and fast. "You don't call me that very often anymore," she said unsteadily.

"Satin suits you better," he replied. His big, warm hands slid under her back and while he held her eyes, he eased the zipper of her dress down to her waist.

"John..." she protested gently, catching the hard fingers that were about to push down the bodice. "I...I'm not wearing anything under the top," she whispered.

"I know," he said, his mustache curling into a devilish smile.

"You said you didn't like doing things half-way," she reminded him.

"Maybe I changed my mind. Let go." He moved her protesting fingers and held her eyes while he dragged the top down to her waist. He looked at her then, and she felt the look all the way to her toes. Her breath caught in her throat at the expression on his dark face as he studied every line, every curve of her bareness with his unblinking gaze.

"Will I pass?" she managed.

"You're so beautiful," he said in a tone that was breathlessly tender. He looked up, holding her in the curve of one arm while his fingers came down on her bare skin. She jumped, gasping, at the new contact.

"Don't be afraid of it," he coaxed, tracing the soft, pale honey curves with fingers that worshipped her high, firm breasts. "We've known each other for a long time."

She could hardly breathe at all. "You've never . . . touched me," she whispered.

"I've wanted to," he said fervently. "Like this. And like this," he whispered, bending to smooth the exquisitely creamy flesh with his lips.

She moaned involuntarily, her hands catching in his thick, dark hair as she tried to decide whether to push or pull.

"You taste of roses," he murmured gruffly, sliding his hands under her again to lift her closer to his hungry lips. "Roses and honey and the sweetest kind of candy. God, Satin, I could eat you!"

She felt his teeth nip her gently, and she arched up, taut and trembling, like a creamy sacrifice, her heart beating so frantically she thought she might die.

His mouth slid up her body until it found her lips, and he eased his warm, hard torso down against her bareness, the faint dampness of the curling hair on his chest cooling her heated skin as she felt him, heavy and sensuous, against her.

Her arms held him, and it was as close to paradise as she'd ever been. She savored the closeness with a pleasure so pure that it hurt.

His mouth slid against her cheek, down to her ear, and she felt a shudder go through him.

"John?" she whispered, concerned.

He turned on the sofa, taking her with him, and pressed her against the powerful length of his body, urging her into its hard contours, as he kissed her again—a long, slow sweet kiss.

She felt the trembling of his body, the inescapable signs of its aching need, and she returned the kiss as gently as he gave it. Against her bareness, his skin was blazing hot, the curling mat of hair tickling, his mustache brushing her mouth.

"You need me...very badly, don't you?" she managed at last, her eyes looking straight into his.

"I can handle it," he said tersely. But the strain was in his face, in the slight trembling of the big arms holding her.

She drew in a slow, steadying breath. She was so full of new emotions, she felt as if she were going to burst open. She wanted nothing more out of life than to give him what he needed so desperately.

"Are you really . . . too tired?" she asked in a voice that sounded blurry.

"I'm tired, all right," he said unsteadily. "But that's going to be a blessing, because I'll have to take a long time with you." He kissed her softly, tenderly, "Oh, God, let me have you, baby," he whispered huskily. "Let me love you. Let me show you the pleasure it can be when two people . . . care about each other."

She trembled against him. "I only want to please you," she said softly. "I want to give you . . . everything."

"And I want to give you everything," he whispered into her mouth. "I don't want sex. I want to make love. I want to possess you, and be possessed by you. To take and be taken. Total union, mind, body, soul . . . with you, only with you . . . !" His mouth ground into hers and he trembled wildly with the force of his own hunger. She held him tenderly, her body yielding, her mind accepting him, wanting him—loving him! There was no room for fear or second thoughts now.

"Only with you," she echoed, and her words were swallowed up in the sound of the pounding rain. He moved, lifting her, and she reached up to press her lips gently against his as he carried her down the long, dark hall into his bedroom, and closed the door.

Chapter Six

It was still raining when Madeline's cab turned off the Loop onto the street where she lived. She leaned forward, her eyes peering worriedly at the downed limbs and scattered lumber.

"Is this becoming a new construction site?" she laughed shakily, taking in the evidence of the night's violent storm.

"Had some bad wind last night," the elderly cabdriver remarked. "And lightning with it. Speaking of lightning, bet it did that. What a mess!" he added, nodding toward the little yellow Volkswagen which had been crushed under the fallen trunk of a mighty oak that was now resting in the middle of Madeline's living room.

"Oh, no!" she groaned. Her fingers clutched the little purse that matched her gold gown. "Oh, no, that's my house! Please...uh, please just stop here, I'll walk across the street. How much do I owe you?"

He told her, his weathered face sympathetic, and watched her run across the rain-wet street with a shake of his head.

She felt tears mingling with the rain on her cheeks as she gaped at the destruction. The car was a total loss. Her house didn't look much more salvageable.

She wasn't a weak woman; she'd weathered worse disasters than this, including the death of her father. But the world looked black just now, and she wished with all her heart that John Durango were there instead of jetting his way to a business conference in Denver.

With a sob, she wrapped her arms around herself, staring at the crushed front of the house. John had warned her about that tree. The trunk was split, as if by a mighty hand, and it was obviously going to take more than her two hands to repair the damage.

"Madeline!"

She turned, to see Donald Durango approaching her from Miss Rose's house next door. With a sob, she ran right into his arms.

"Thank God!" he breathed. "I've been out of my mind. Where were you?"

Now there was a question, and she wasn't about to answer it. "Never mind that," she moaned. "Look at my house. Look at my poor little car! Oh, Donald . . . !" She wiped her eyes. "I was going to go inside and make myself a cup of coffee," she said bewilderedly, staring at the house blankly. Shock made her numb all over.

"Come on home with me," he suggested. "I've got that garage apartment, and I won't be needing it as a studio for a while. You can have it until you get that roof fixed. And the tree removed from your living room," he added with a faint smile. "Everything's going to be all right."

"My car . . . !" She wept.

"You needed a new one, anyway," he said. "The engine in that one was shot."

"It wasn't," she grumbled, scowling. "It had at least another hundred miles on it."

"You've been spending too much time around John," he pointed out. "It's only good for junk."

She looked down at her dress. "I don't have any clothes with me."

"Stay here. I'll rummage around inside and get you a few things. Looks like the tree only got the living room. Everything else should be fairly safe."

"Should you go in there?" she asked uncertainly. "I don't want you to get hurt for a few clothes. I could buy something."

"I'll be okay."

"Miss Rose..." she said, suddenly worried, her eyes going to the house next door.

"Is fine," he told her. "I ran over there like a wild man a few minutes ago when I finally decided to drive over here and see if you were okay." He sighed with heartfelt relief. "I'd been calling you all night and getting no answer. Miss Rose said you'd been picked up yesterday by a man in a Ferrari and hadn't come back." He studied her suddenly flushed face. "An observant lady, Miss Rose. And an incurable romantic. She's convinced that you and John ran away and got married."

She felt hot all over at just the thought of it. "Uh, not exactly," she hedged, averting her eyes.

"Well, it's not any of *my* business, after all," he returned, but his eyes were curious. "I'll see what I can salvage."

She stood there in the cold rain and watched him go, her mind whirling. The shock had been tremendous, and she still felt numb. To come from John's warm bed to this....

Her eyes closed and she tried not to remember how it had been last night. She could still feel John's hands under her back, gently lifting; and his mouth against her soft, bare skin with the mustache like a velvet brush over every inch of it. The feel of his taut, powerful body against hers, the man scent of him, the husky sound of his voice as he whispered urgently, ardently, at her throat....

Everything had changed between them by morning: everything, including the easy camaraderie of the past. This morning he'd been strangely reticent, and she'd been wary of him, frankly shy of his penetrating gaze as she'd huddled under the brown sheets and the chocolate and cream striped bedspread.

"We'll talk when I get back from Denver," he'd said.

"Yes," she'd replied quietly, and he'd put her in a cab and gone back inside the apartment house without glancing back at her....

"I said, are you ready to go?" Donald asked, indicating the suitcase in his hand. "I closed off the rooms that weren't damaged, so the rain wouldn't get in. It's only the living room, and it shouldn't be all that difficult to repair. The biggest job will be getting the tree removed."

"I'll, uh, I'll call someone about it later," she said. Her dress was dripping wet and clinging unpleasantly to her body. "I'd like to get into something dry."

"Let's go, then. I parked over at Miss Rose's."

She followed him blindly, pausing just long enough to smile and talk briefly with Miss Rose, who was delighted to find her alive and overtly curious about where she'd been. Madeline sidestepped the question diplomatically and eased away before Miss Rose realized that she hadn't been answered.

"Where were you, really?" Donald probed, his eyes speculative as they drove back to his house. "Not with John all night—I know you too well to believe that."

If only you knew the truth, she thought, laughing inside. But she shrugged and gave him a slightly forced smile. "Wouldn't you like to know?" she murmured. "Maybe I was out committing a murder—doing research for my next book."

He sighed dramatically. "And now you've just made me an accomplice after the fact."

"I know a good attorney who'll defend us both," she said.

He chuckled. "I'll just bet you do."

She leaned back in the seat. "Thanks for offering me the use of your apartment. Are you sure you don't need it for visiting ... friends?" she teased.

"What do you think you are?"

"I know what I'm going to be when John Durango finds out where I am," she moaned, closing her eyes. He would be livid, she knew that already, and with their relationship on new and shaky ground, she didn't know how she was going to explain it to him.

"Miss Rose did offer you a room in her house," Donald pointed out, his blue eyes teasing.

"Miss Rose is a member of the War Widows Historical Society," she told him.

"So?"

She turned in the seat. "So, they don't just reminisce about the war, sometimes they reenact it."

He blinked. "With horses and sabers and everything?" he asked pleasantly.

"Oh, don't be silly," she muttered. "Not *that* war!"

"Which one, then?" he asked.

"World War I," she said. "And they remember it with very loud poetry and rousing battle songs and such. Little old ladies rushing about on horses waving sabers...!" She muffled a giggle at the very thought.

"Knowing Miss Rose," he countered, "I wouldn't be a bit surprised."

Honestly, neither would I, she thought, but didn't say it out loud. She'd wanted to take Miss Rose up on the offer, she really had. But if she did, it would be like admitting that she was afraid of John's reaction to her living at Donald's estate. And, too, with all the commotion of the weekly War Widows meetings, she'd never be able to get any writing done. Miss Rose was a talker; even when she wasn't talking, she was listening to her programs on the radio with the volume as loud as it would go because she was half-deaf. Her local news shows and the obituaries were something she didn't miss, not ever.

So it had been Donald's garage apartment or a motel. And there was no way she was going to give John that kind of satisfaction. He didn't own her, not even after a night like the one they'd just shared. She wasn't about to be added to his list of possessions, as she'd already told him.

The garage apartment was only a stone's throw from the rear entrance of Donald's sprawling brick home, just the right size for a single tenant. It consisted of a large, studio-type living room with a foldout bed, a full bath, and a combination kitchen-dining room. The living room was rather cluttered with paints and easels but Madeline didn't mind. She expected to be doing too much writing to worry about the decor.

She unpacked the suitcase Donald had filled, groaning at the obvious omissions. He'd put in slacks, blouses, and even a couple of wrinkle-free dresses—but no underthings. Just like a bachelor, she thought amusedly, not to consider what went under clothes. As soon as she had transportation, she'd have to rectify that problem. And she'd just noticed that Donald hadn't remembered her typewriter, either. That did it. She had to have a car so she could get around on her own.

She changed into her jeans and a blue T-shirt and, after pausing to make a few phone calls, went next door to see Donald.

"May I use one of your cars for a little while?" she asked without preamble, her face worried.

"I've got to start looking for a replacement for my Volkswagen."

"What's the rush?" Donald asked. "You can borrow the Lincoln as long as you're staying here."

"Too big," she sighed, shaking her head, but the real reason for her refusal was a reluctance to depend on anyone other than herself. "Look, I've got to have transportation. How about going car shopping with me—if you can spare the time?"

"For you, anything." He stopped long enough to tell his housekeeper where he'd be, and escorted Madeline out to the big Lincoln. "Hop in," he said gaily. "What kind of car did you have in mind—a Fiat, a Ferrari . . ."

"A VW," she said firmly.

He stared at her across the seat. "You're not an impoverished writer on a budget these days, you know," he teased.

"I like VWs," she replied. "They're good on gas, they have good acceleration, and they're cute."

"God deliver me, the last thing I look for in a car is cuteness."

"I think Lincolns are cute," she informed him.

He started the car. "Let's go, for heaven's sake, before you start talking to it."

She finally found what she wanted on the sixth car lot Donald drove her to—a little yellow VW that was almost a dead ringer for the one she'd lost; except that it was five years younger and didn't have dents in the rear fenders.

"This?" Donald exclaimed, scowling at it.

"Don't insult my new car," she defended, patting its little roof. "Isn't it cute?"

Donald just shook his head. "Have you called the insurance people about your old one?" he asked.

"Of course. I called the repair people, too, they should already be out there."

"Excuse me for prying into your business, but didn't you think about getting some estimates first?" he asked.

"I've known Bill Gonnells most of my life," she laughed. "We went to school together. He's a building contractor. And fortunately he could do it."

"I know Bill, too, he's responsible for that garage apartment you're living in right now," he told her with a smile. "How about the tree?"

"The Civil Defense people have to get it off the power lines it dragged down," she said. "They're going to take the lumber and raffle it off for firewood to buy a Hurst Tool for the emergency unit."

"Son of a gun," he murmured. "You are efficient, aren't you?"

"Well, I didn't need the wood," she said. "And it's for a worthy cause—and I promised to do the press release."

"You and your causes," he sighed.

"Old reporters never get out of the habit," she told him. "I have the greatest kind of respect for volunteer firemen, policemen and rescue service workers. They train on their own time, buy their own equipment, and are on call twenty-four hours a day. The paid workers are just as dedicated, too."

"Do you often tilt at windmills?" he teased.

"Only once a day," she said. "I'm getting older, you know."

She went by the house to pick up her typewriter and notes, weaving her way through disaster crews and the contracting crew with a grateful smile. Her little yellow Volkswagen, the old one, had been uncovered, its pitiful roof like a crushed melon. It would have to be towed away and junked, and it was like losing an old friend.

She paused to lay a hand on its crumpled fender, remembering her amusement the first time

John had tried to drive it; and the day he was haying, when he'd climbed in beside her and kissed her so hungrily.

Frowning, she moved away into the house and made short work of gathering the things she needed. Minutes later, she was on her way.

Two days went by without a word from John, while Madeline sat at the typewriter and tried doggedly to work out character sketches and locations for the sequel to *The Grinding Tower.* Her schedule had been badly interrupted for over a week, and it was hellish going back to it.

In some ways it had been easier when she wrote at night, after she came home from the newspaper office. She'd budgeted her time more wisely then. After she had quit and come home to work on her novels full-time, she'd fallen into bad habits, the worst of which was driving to the post office early each morning to get the mail. That meant she didn't get started until late morning, and the lunch break managed to play havoc with her concentration.

Memories were doing that, too. Memories of that long, stormy night in John Durango's arms.

She leaned over the typewriter, her thoughts straying, her body tingling as she thought back. Even though she was inexperienced with men, she couldn't help thinking that he'd been like a man who hadn't had a woman in a very long time. He'd been tender and patient, keeping a tight rein on himself until he'd roused her—so that she held back nothing when they finally, slowly, merged together. But he'd been rigid with the force of holding himself in check; he'd been bathed in sweat. And the second time, he'd been reckless, passionate, totally out of control—he'd apologized for it, and she'd found that strange, too.

She hadn't expected the wild, anguished pleasure he'd shown her. The memory of pain had been strong, and her faint fear of him had made her fight at first. But his voice had soothed her, his hands had gentled her, and with an expertise that still could take her breath, he'd stroked and touched and kissed her until she'd begged him to end the exquisite torment.

He hadn't taunted her with her absolute surrender, either, or laughed at her for pleading with him. He'd cherished her like a priceless delicacy, nibbling and savoring her until dawn peeked through the curtains after the night of rain and wind and lightning.

He had barely an hour's sleep before the alarm clock woke them with its urgent, shrill jangle, summoning John to his business meeting in Denver. Half-asleep, she'd watched him dress with swift, economical motions, too shy to climb out of the bed under his watchful eyes. He'd sensed that, and without a word, he'd left her alone to dress.

They'd barely exchanged ten words when he put her in a cab, and guilt and regret and a strange anxiety were all mirrored in his silver eyes as she left.

She shook her head, staring at the single paragraph that amounted to a morning's work. He'd been so different the night before. So tender, so caring....

"Don't let me hurt you," he'd whispered, his voice taut with desire, his hands slow and gentle as they lifted her, guided her. "I want it to be perfect between us. Absolutely... perfect."

"It's beautiful," she'd whispered back, her voice splintering with the force of her own emotions. Then new sensations had ripped into her with a pleasure bordering on madness.

She closed her eyes, shivering with the memory. She'd never dreamed it was possible to experience that kind of pleasure and live. For the first time in her life, she understood why the French called lovemaking the little death.

She got up and covered the typewriter. This was getting her nowhere. How was she going to write with John imbedded in her mind?

She gave up and fixed herself a grilled cheese sandwich and a cup of coffee. Perhaps later she could recapture her muse.

But later and still later, she hadn't gotten past that single paragraph. It was after nine o'clock. She covered the typewriter again and went to take a shower. She might as well have an early night and get some sleep.

The stinging shower spray felt good on her skin. She lathered herself with a floral soap and closed her eyes, feeling once again the long, slow caress of John's hands, the sound of his deep voice whispering as he told her how exquisite she looked to those glittering, silver eyes in the soft glow of the bedside lamp they'd forgotten to turn off....

She rinsed herself irritably. She didn't want to remember. Now that she'd given in once, he'd expect it as his due, and it was only one step from there to possession. She wouldn't become his mistress, she wouldn't! Despite the fact that she had little family left, there was a streak of old-fashioned morality in her that wouldn't let her accept such a relationship with him. It had been bad enough to give in to those raging fires he'd kindled. She wouldn't flaunt her weakness in front of all Houston.

She stepped out of the shower and dried herself on the fluffy blue towel, removing the frilly shower cap to let her red gold hair flow in waves around her white shoulders.

Part of her was still wondering how she was going to explain her residence here to John when he got home from Denver. Knowing how he felt about Donald, even if she didn't completely understand why, she was going to find it difficult to justify her actions. Of course, she reasoned, she was a big girl now. And despite her growing...fondness...for John, he didn't own her. She wasn't going to let that happen.

Fondness. She stood, the towel held loosely in her hands, pondering that word. It didn't have a lot to do with her gnawing hunger to please him, to give, to share with him. What she felt was something she'd never experienced, something nameless.

She shook back her long hair with a frown. This was getting her nowhere.

Still brooding, she walked out of the bathroom into the bedroom/living room stark naked, the towel trailing listlessly from one hand. There was suddenly a loud slam, footsteps, and before the thought really registered that she had company, the apartment door was flung open and John Durango walked in, fury in every hard line of his face.

Chapter Seven

Madeline gaped at him, oblivious for a split second to her state of undress.

"Expecting my cousin?" he demanded coldly, and his silver eyes touched every inch of her in expert appraisal.

Belatedly, she fumbled the towel around her with cold, trembling fingers.

"I...I wasn't expecting anyone," she said nervously.

"What the hell are you doing here?" he wanted to know, his tone the same one he probably used at board meetings when he was cutting up a subordinate.

She drew herself up proudly, her hair falling in waves around her bare shoulders, her eyes a vivid green in her flushed face. "What the hell business is it of yours?" she replied.

"You can ask me that, after what we shared?" he breathed furiously.

The flush grew hotter and she averted her eyes.

"Did you think you'd own me after one night?" she asked harshly.

"Stop answering questions with questions," he growled. He made a rough gesture with one big hand, reached for a cigarette, found his pocket empty and mumbled something she was glad she didn't understand.

"Have you been by my house?" she asked, clutching the towel closer. "Do you know what happened?"

"Yes, I've been by your house," he muttered, and for the first time she noticed that he looked strangely pale. "You might have left a note on the door," he added tautly. "I had to drag Miss Rose out of bed to find out if you were alive. Which shocked her," he continued angrily, "because she seemed to have the distinct impression that we were planning to elope."

She avoided his eyes. "Miss Rose is a hopeless romantic," she faltered. The tone of his voice had hurt, as if marriage to her was unthinkable.

"Couldn't you have managed a minute to call and tell Josito?"

"I'm sorry," she said, subdued. "I've been too upset to do much thinking. I had to buy another car, and arrange for repairs . . . and someplace to live," she added, lifting her eyes to his. "A tree went through the roof!"

"There was no tree through the roof when I drove buy," he countered.

"Of course not, the rescue people have removed it!"

"You aren't making a hell of a lot of sense," he observed. "And you still haven't told me why you're here!"

"Why should I?" she shot back. "I'm free, single and over twenty-one, and nobody, but *nobody*, tells me what to do anymore!"

"Think so?" he replied, smiling coolly.

"I know so!" She shifted uncomfortably. "John, I don't want to fight with you."

"Are you living with him?" he asked.

Her temper went wild. "I most certainly am not! For heaven's sake, what would people think . . . !"

"They're already thinking it," he informed her coldly. "Or did you imagine no one would notice?"

Her eyes closed on a wave of embarrassment. "I had to have someplace to live," she muttered.

"What was wrong with Miss Rose's house?"

"The War Widows Historical Society, that's what!"

"You could move in with me," he returned.

She went pale at the thought. Living with him, being with him, sitting down to meals with him, watching him around the house, sharing his life...

He moved closer, his face still hard, although his eyes softened just a little. His big, warm hands caught her bare shoulders and held her just in front of him while he studied her.

"Don't...do that," she whispered unsteadily. His callused hands made magic where they touched.

"Live with me," he whispered. He bent, touching his hard mouth to hers, kissing it softly while she struggled to maintain any sanity at all.

"I can't," she breathed.

"You want to," he countered. "Don't you?" He lifted her in his big arms while his mouth nibbled at her parted lips, his teeth nipping them gently, his smoky breath mingling with hers as he walked toward the bed. "Do you remember how it was, Madeline?" he whispered sensuously. "You begged me . . ."

"No!" She struggled with him, hating her own weakness, hating his easy victory. All he had to do was touch her and she capitulated!

"Yes," he ground out against her mouth. She felt the bed under her back, John's huge body pressing her deep into the mattress as his hungry mouth invaded hers and knocked the resistance right out of her.

She felt herself go deliciously limp as his hands smoothed away the towel and made slow, sweet patterns against her bare back, her hips, her thighs.

"You're . . . heavy," she whispered shakily when he finally lifted his mouth from her swollen lips.

"It's all these damned clothes," he murmured with a faint smile, "not me." He kissed her closed eyelids, her nose, her cheeks, the corner of her mouth. "You smell of wildflowers," he whispered. "And you taste like honey." His breathing quickened as he shifted, letting his lips wander down her throat, over her collarbone, onto the silken skin of her shoulders and lower, to softly rounded flesh that tautened traitorously under the caress. "Help me undress," he whispered sensuously.

Her fingers reached up to hold his face so that she could see his eyes. They were dark with desire, smoldering.

"We've got to talk," she said in a trembling voice, her body tingling, aching, from the total contact with his.

"We can do a better job of it without words," he murmured gruffly. His long forefinger traced the soft line of her mouth, his eyes studying it intently. "Oh, God, I missed you! All I could think about the whole time was how it was between us, the feel of your skin against mine, those sweet, wild little cries...."

"Don't!" she groaned, turning her face away as the memory made her want to cry.

He tautened above her, then forced her to look at him again. "You're ashamed of it," he whispered incredulously.

Her eyes closed. Her mouth trembled. "Yes, I'm ashamed," she ground out. "Let me go, John. Please."

Without another word, he rolled away and got to his feet with the grace of a big cat. He stared at her as she rewrapped the towel and sat up, her face the shade of dawn roses.

His hands were jammed deep in his pockets, his eyes glaring at her. "Talk to me, damn it! What was there to be ashamed of?"

She stared down at the carpet, hating herself, hating him. "We had something rare," she managed. "And it all fell apart. Why did you do it?" Her voice broke. "Why did you have to spoil it!"

"I didn't rape you," he reminded her, his voice icy.

Her eyes closed. "No," she admitted, "you didn't. You just took advantage of what I felt for you. You're just like every other man, John Durango, you only care about what you can get! I'm surprised that you had the patience to wait two years for me, when there were so many Melodys around, just dying to give out!"

His face paled under its tan. His big body tensed. "Was that all it meant to you?"

She laughed mirthlessly. "What else?" she asked, although it tore her heart open to dismiss that devastating beauty in two contemptuous words. She couldn't let him see how vulnerable she was, she couldn't wind up as just another conquest to be enjoyed for a little while, and then tossed aside. He'd said for years that he'd never marry again. Not that she wanted to marry him, she told herself stubbornly.

"How did you wind up here?" he asked after a minute, glaring at the surroundings. "Was he sitting on the porch waiting for you?"

She sighed wearily. "I got home to find my car crushed and a tree in the middle of my living room. You were on your way to Denver and Donald was sitting on Miss Rose's porch waiting for me. He offered me a home; what could I say?"

"How about 'no, thanks'?" he suggested coldly. "You've flaunted your relationship with my cousin ever since you first met him. I've tolerated it because of our friendship. But living on his doorstep is something else. I can't take that."

"Your trust is overwhelming," she ground out.

"It isn't a question of trust," he said, and he sounded bone tired. "I thought we had something more permanent going for us than a casual night together. But you quite obviously don't share that opinion. You know what my cousin is, and how he feels about you. If you're willing to live this close to him, you must share those feelings. I've tried not to believe it, but it's too obvious now to ignore."

"I don't have buried desires for Donald!" she threw back.

"Prove it," he challenged. "Move in with me."

She lifted her head proudly. "No."

"And that says it all, doesn't it?" His eyes glittered at her, smoldering with anger barely held in check. "You've chosen him over me."

"That's not true!" she cried, standing up. "John, it isn't that kind of arrangement. I'm not sleeping with him, I'm not!"

His angry gaze went up and down her with a contempt that made her want to go through the floor. "You, and my cousin..." he grated venomously.

"Donald," she corrected. "His name is Donald, why won't you ever use it...?"

"Did I hear my name called?" Donald paused in the doorway, wearing a dressing gown over his pajamas; he had a bottle of champagne and two glasses in his hands, a wicked grin on his face. "Sorry I took so long, darling...."

John seemed to explode. His fist shot out and Donald went flying to land heavily in the middle of the carpet. The glasses crashed around him, followed by the thud of the champagne bottle which, miraculously, remained unbroken.

"Now, Cousin John, was that polite?" Donald groaned, rubbing his jaw.

John didn't even answer him. His accusing gaze was on Madeline's white, disbelieving face. There was a contempt in his face she'd never seen as his eyes made an insulting sweep of her body in the towel, then darted back to Donald. Without a word, he turned and went out the door.

Madeline clutched her towel, her eyes accusing as they lit on Donald.

"What possessed you?" she asked coldly, indicating the mess around him.

"I heard him asking Maisie where you were, and I thought it would be nice to make friendly overtures," he said, grinning.

"Toward whom?" she countered.

"Don't be cross, sweet, it was one of those impulses I get occasionally to needle old Cousin John." He chuckled. "Did you see his face? Whew! I feel fortunate to have come away with only a few loosened teeth and a dislocated jaw."

"Would you mind taking the remains of your vulgar impulse out of my room?" she asked quietly. She felt as numb as if she'd died.

He cocked an eyebrow at her. "We could still drink the champagne. Or, if you'd rather," he added with a strange leer, "we could bathe in it together."

She walked to the closet and pulled on a robe over her towel. "Good night, Donald."

He picked up the champagne bottle with a sigh, his expression regretful. "I'll have the mess cleaned up in the morning. Mind the glass. Good night."

But she didn't reply. When he was gone, she climbed into bed in her robe and lay there with hot tears streaming down her cheeks. Why hadn't she realized when she gave in to John that night that it would ruin what they'd had?

No more lazy days riding horseback with him. No more evenings at the ballet, or watching that television star who looked like him once a week. No more telephone calls late at night just because he was lonely and needed to talk. It was like giving up part of her life, a part that had come to mean everything to her, she realized.

Would it have been so terrible to live with him, on his terms? To spend every night in his warm, protective arms? To share everything with him?

She buried her face in the pillow. Well, it was too late now, her pride had seen to that. Rather than admit that she was in love with him, she'd forced him out of her life, and John wasn't the kind of man to come running back. He was too proud.

Love. Four letters, one word that had managed to change the world and everything in it. She loved John. Why, oh, why hadn't she known that before she let him carry her to bed? Why hadn't she seen it coming?

Well, it was too late now. John thought she was two-timing him with his despised cousin, and he'd never forgive her. So she had her precious freedom, her independence. And it was as empty as her life was going to be without John Durango in it.

She got up the next morning and dressed mechanically in a white sheath dress to meet her policeman friend. She looked ghostly, her face pale, her eyes dull, but skillfully applied makeup restored the bloom to her complexion.

On her way to the little yellow Volkswagen, she met Donald, who had obviously come out of the house to intercept her.

"Good morning," he said. "Sorry about last night. Are you okay?"

She couldn't resist that smile, even though she'd wanted to kill him hours before. "Yes, I'm okay," she replied. "It's just as well, I suppose. John and I weren't seeing eye to eye anyway lately."

"That's my girl. Where are you off to?"

"Reno's," she replied, naming a downtown restaurant in Houston's vast office plaza with its avenue of shops and underground garage. "I'm doing research on the next book."

He frowned slightly. "I suppose you know that's one of Cousin John's watering holes?" he asked quietly.

She blanched. The last thing in the world she wanted was to run into John now. But it was too late to call Sergeant Mulligan and change the meeting place; she was due there in just ten minutes. She'd have to chance it.

"My, what a thoughtful expression," he mused.

She laughed mirthlessly. "I'm not thinking, I'm praying. How was the champagne, by the way?"

"Delicious. The whole bottle. Well, good luck."

"Thanks," she murmured. "I may need it."

Madeline had met Sergeant Jack Mulligan during her stint as a reporter, and he'd been an invaluable source of information ever since. He worked in the homicide investigation department and he'd forgotten more about police work than most rookies had learned. Except for confidential information or current cases, he didn't mind sharing what he knew.

"I can't tell you how much I appreciate this," Madeline told him over a plate of spaghetti, after an hour of intense questions about a particular case she was interested in. "Especially on your day off."

Mulligan only smiled, his grizzled face hard from all the sights and sounds that the public rarely witnessed. He smoothed back his silver hair. "My pleasure. I've never forgotten that book you dedicated to me. My wife drags it out every time we have a visitor."

"That was the least I could do." She sipped her coffee, her eyes surveying the restaurant every time someone new walked in.

"Anything else you need?" he asked.

"As a matter of fact," she murmured, smiling, "I could use some information on drug dealing in the city. I'm using a drug ring as background, and I want to be as accurate as possible. I've had a lot of cooperation from the Drug Enforcement Administration on it—they've been great. But I need some more detailed information on the local scene. I want to know what it's like for a policeman who goes undercover."

"Simple," he said. "First he stops shaving and bathing, then he adopts a glazed expression and learns how to fake toking on a reefer."

She blinked at him, her fork poised in midair over the plate of barely touched spaghetti in its rich, thick red sauce. "I beg your pardon?"

He put down his fork. "Okay, madam detective, this is how it goes...."

He slowly went through the structure of the narcotics organization—right down to the types of marijuana, where they came from, how they were imported, who sold the drug, who bought it, and how to smoke it. Madeline feverishly jotted down the information in her black notebook, hoping that she'd be able to decipher the scribbles later. It was too involved to memorize.

"Fascinating, isn't it?" he asked finally. "It still fascinates me, and I've worked the streets for twenty years. It's a dirty business, and the dirtiest part is when you realize how many fine, upstanding citizens are financing it. The roots of corruption are thick and deep, and it's a constant battle trying to clip them. The tragedy is that most of the pushers are well known to police—even some of the sources. But you can't arrest a man without evidence, and getting it is an uphill battle."

"Getting an indictment isn't too difficult, is it?" she asked.

"Nope. But getting a conviction is," he said with a world-weary smile. "You can spend weeks building a chain of evidence to arrest a pusher, have him arraigned and brought to trial—only to have a sympathetic jury turn him loose on some technicality."

"Which is why policemen cry in their beer?" she murmured.

"Not exactly. We just work harder." He sipped his coffee. "That reminds me, the rescue boys were really tickled about that wood you donated for their firewood raffle."

"I hope it goes over. A firewood raffle in late spring . . ."

"Oh, they won't hold the raffle until fall," he corrected. He grinned. "They'll stack up that firewood and let it age through the summer."

She laughed. "I should have known." The smile faded as she looked up straight into the flashing eyes of the big, craggy-faced man in a pale gray vested suit and matching Stetson, who was just walking in the door with three other businessmen.

"Uh-oh," she whispered.

Sergeant Mulligan followed her stare. "Friend of yours?" he asked.

"Good question," she replied.

John Durango excused himself from his companions and strode toward Madeline's table, hat in hand. He looked like impending doom, and she braced herself for trouble. Surely he wouldn't make a scene!

"What the hell kind of games are you playing?" he asked without preamble, glancing only momentarily at her companion. "I told you it was over, why are you deliberately following me?"

She gasped. "Following you?"

"How else can you explain your presence in my favorite restaurant?" he growled, and his eyes were contemptuous.

"I am having lunch with a friend," she said coldly. "Not chasing after you. I do not chase after conceited men who think they are God's gift to women."

"You're not very selective, are you?" he asked, glaring at Mulligan. "Isn't he a little old for you?"

"Don't let the gray hair fool you, son, I just graduated from high school," Mulligan said dryly.

John wasn't amused. At that moment he looked as if he hadn't smiled in his life. He glared at Madeline.

"Since you were desperate enough to come looking for me, we might as well talk." He pulled up a chair and sat down, tossing his Stetson on the empty seat next to Madeline. "Get rid of your friend, and we'll discuss it."

"I will not, and there's nothing to discuss," she shot at him, hurting deep inside at his coldness. Once, John wouldn't have dreamed of speaking to her like that, or suspecting her of being promiscuous. Now he was looking at her as if she'd opened up shop as a hooker.

"No?" John sized up Mulligan. "Are you another one of those underworld characters she pumps for information?"

"He is not!" Madeline gasped, glaring at him. "I don't know any underworld characters!"

"Oh, no? What about that retired smuggler you used to write to?"

"Will you shut up?" she squeaked, glancing apprehensively at Mulligan, who was trying to smother a grin.

"It wouldn't surprise me if you had a hit man somewhere in your retinue of acquaintances—" John glared at her. "You know the worst kind of rabble!"

"Well, your friends aren't the cream of society either," she threw back. "What about that evil-smelling drunk who came to my dinner party with you at Christmas?''

"He was my father's first rigger, and what you smelled was some cologne of mine he borrowed!" He drew in an angry breath. "And he was not drunk!''

"What would you call it?" she asked hotly, glowering. "He tried to feed liver pâté to my Norfolk Island pine!''

"He was trying to dispose of the damned stuff so he wouldn't have to eat it," he informed her.

"You ate yours!''

"Like hell I did, I stuffed it in my pocket," he grumbled.

She gasped. "I spent hours making it!''

"Josito spend hours trying to get it out of my coat pocket," he informed her.

She glared across at him, her eyes sparking. She hated his arrogance, hated his impeccable neatness. Not a hair out of place, as usual, and two women at a nearby table were openly leering at him.

"This is getting us nowhere," he said after a minute, his tone curt. "Have lunch with me and let's talk about last night.''

"I don't want to have lunch with you," she informed him.

"But you're going to," he said in his usual commanding way.

She smiled tightly. "If you insist. Here, I'll let you share mine."

And, still smiling, she picked up her plateful of spaghetti and poured it slowly into his lap, watching the red tomato sauce ooze down over the pale fabric of his expensive suit pants.

Jack Mulligan was still laughing when they got to the parking lot underneath the restaurant, tears of mirth in his eyes.

"I'll never forget the look on Durango's face," he managed. "Remind me never to upset you, lady."

She laughed, too, now that it was over. "I don't know which was worse, the spaghetti sauce or finding out what you did for a living after those nasty remarks he made. And I don't know any hit men," she added with a quick, sideways glance.

"I'm glad to hear it," he chuckled. "Sorry about your lunch. Would you like to go somewhere else and try again?"

She shook her head. "Thanks anyway, but my appetite's gone. I really appreciate what you've done for me, Jack. If I can ever do anything for you..."

"You already did," he grinned. "I haven't laughed so much in months."

Later, transcribing her notes in the garage apartment, she wondered if it had been such a good idea to ignore John's overtures. Perhaps he'd meant to apologize for his accusations. Perhaps he'd wanted to make up.

Or maybe he'd just wanted to get her back to bed. That was what hurt the most, the thought that she might be nothing more than another woman to him: one he was temporarily, but not permanently, interested in. He'd asked her to live with him, of course, but not as his wife. And she'd slowly arrived at the conclusion that what she wanted most in the world was to share her life with John; to bear his children, to love him as long as she was alive. But she didn't want to be relegated to a hidden corner, like some shameful habit that he didn't want openly acknowledged. She couldn't survive being his mistress, not feeling this way about him.

With a heavy sigh, she got up from her makeshift desk and stared out the window at Donald's house next door. At this rate, John would finish her off before she finished the book. She couldn't remember a time in her life when things had looked so dark, so empty. All she could foresee for herself now was loneliness.

That depression lasted for days, and it took all her willpower not to call Josito and find out if John was in town. It wouldn't have mattered anyway; he wasn't going to call her. He'd made that perfectly obvious. Probably, she thought miserably, he was escorting Melody around town and hadn't even minded that Madeline was out of his life for good. After all, there were plenty of women trying to get into his bed. Now she'd joined those ranks herself, and he had only contempt for the easy way she'd given in to him. Probably he'd lost every bit of respect he ever had for her.

Friday night, Donald, clearly seeing the desperation in her troubled eyes, invited her to go to a disco with him.

"You'll love it," he promised. "They serve a great steak supper, and the music's loud enough to make you forget your name. It's brand new and a favorite hangout for the young crowd."

She eyed him. "How young?"

He looked briefly uncomfortable. "If we wear the right clothes, no one will even notice."

"Hey, thanks a lot," she grumbled. "Do I look *that* old?"

"We're the same age," he pointed out.

She sighed. "And lately I feel about forty. My get up and go has got up and went, as the saying goes. Okay, I'll try it out. I just happen to have this great silver disco dress that I never get a chance to wear. I'll drop by the house and pick it up."

He grinned. "That's my girl!"

It should have occurred to her to wonder why Donald was taking her to a disco when his own musical taste ran to Verdi and Wagner. But it didn't. It was only when they were seated at a table facing the multilighted dance floor with its pulsing colors and throbbing music that his motives became clear. Glancing over her steak and red wine, she noticed John Durango only four tables away, with Melody sitting practically in his lap.

"I will murder you," she told Donald sweetly, her fork poised in midair. "I will sprinkle a beastly, non-detectable poison over your food one night and stand gaily by while you choke and gasp your last!"

"No, you won't," Donald said confidently, sipping his wine with sparkling eyes. "Well, you were mooning over him. I just called Josito and asked where he was—that is, I had Maisie do it. The rest was simple.''

"Just like me," she muttered. "Simple. Well, you can take me home right now!" She threw down her napkin.

"Oh, no, I can't possibly," he said pleasantly, blinking. "You see, if you walk out that door, he'll know that you're jealous."

"I'm not . . ." She lowered her voice. "I'm not jealous."

He grinned. "Yes, you are."

She felt eyes boring into her, and looked up straight into John's silver gaze. He was openly glaring, and the impact of his look made her heart turn over. His mouth under the mustache was drawn into a thin line, and his face was rigid. She dropped her eyes quickly to the remains of her steak, wishing her renegade heart would slow down.

"My, my, what a wicked glare that was," Donald chuckled. "Furious, isn't he?"

"You know very well I'd walk a mile to avoid John right now," she ground out.

"The reverse is also true, if my cousin's expression is anything to go by," he replied. "And Melody looks as if she might sprout horns any second. Pretty little thing, isn't she? So young, too."

That hurt. She gave Donald her best I'll-get-you-yet stare and watched him wiggle under it. "She's a knockout, all right," she agreed with a sweet smile. "Lucky John."

Donald pursed her lips and studied her. "Strange, that isn't what you said at Elise's party that night. In fact, you did your best to rescue him from her clutches."

"We were friends, then," she replied, and memories of those seemingly long-ago days made her sad. She finished her steak without tasting it, and tossed back her red gold hair after she demolished the rest of the wine. The silver disco dress glittered as she moved, highlighting the slenderness of her body, the fiery shade of her hair.

"You're still *my* friend, I hope," he said.

She sighed. "I suppose so," she admitted, her eyes soulful. "With a vicious personality like yours, you need at least one friend. How lucky for you that I have the hide of a rhinoceros."

He laughed softly. "And the memory of a six-month-old," he added, teasing. He got to his feet. "Dance with me. We'll show 'em how."

"I'm not even sure I can do that kind of dance," she muttered, letting him lead her away from the table.

"It's easy. You just pretend that you're walking over a row of water moccasins barefooted."

"Uhggg!" she shuddered, trying to look normal as she was led past John's table.

Naturally, Donald stopped just at that moment, and flashed his best grin at John. The older man, in an open-throated white silk shirt under an expensive burgundy velvet jacket, was something to catch any woman's eye.

"Well, well, if it isn't Cousin John," Donald said in mock surprise. "And who's this? Melody, isn't it?" he added with an appreciative look at the little blonde. "Melody, I don't know if you're aware of it, but Madeline here is a great friend of John's," he added wickedly.

"Yes, I know her very well," John replied, and everyone but Madeline missed the double entendre in his words.

"We had lunch together just last week," she told Melody sweetly. "Spaghetti, wasn't it?" she murmured, turning to the other girl's escort.

John cocked an eyebrow at her. "That's what it felt like," he agreed casually.

"I didn't know you cared for disco, cousin," Donald remarked.

John glared at him. "Melody likes it," he said shortly.

Madeline felt her blood start to simmer, but she forced a smile. "Ah, it's so nice for young people, though, isn't it, John?" she asked with a sigh. "Of course, at your age, old friend—" she emphasized the *old* "—this kind of dancing can be dangerous. It could throw your back out for weeks. Not to mention what it can do to arthritic joints."

"I don't have arthritic joints," he pointed out curtly.

"That you know of," she agreed. Her eyes lowered demurely. "But you have been complaining of aches a lot lately."

She felt rather than saw him bristle, and wondered at her own impudence in baiting him. It wasn't going to help the situation.

"I've found a nice remedy for those aches," he replied after a minute, his arm going around Melody, who snuggled close with a smug look at Madeline.

"Let's go, love," Donald said, easing his arm around her waist and grinning at John, whose eyes flashed dangerously. "See you, cousin."

She let Donald lead her onto the dance floor blindly, hurting in ways she'd never imagined she could. She let her body translate its painful rage into movement as she mechanically went through the paces of the disco dances, losing herself in the light and music. Only a little over two weeks ago, she and John had been as close as two people could get, and now they might as well live in different countries. It broke her heart.

She was aware of eyes watching her, and turned to see John and Melody dancing nearby. For a man of his size and age, John was devastating on the dance floor. He put most of the younger men, including Donald, to shame, and hardly had a hair out of place when the music stopped for a few seconds.

One of the younger girls moved close to John and Melody, her big blue eyes fascinated as she stared up at him. "Excuse me," Madeline heard her say, "but aren't you the star of that TV series?"

"Sorry, I'm not," came the amused reply, and he smiled exactly like the adventure series hero he so closely resembled.

"Has anyone ever told you..." the girl persisted.

"... that I sound like him?" John teased. "A few people."

"Well, you sure do!" she sighed. "I'm sorry, I hope I didn't embarrass you."

"Not at all," John replied with another rugged grin.

Madeline lifted her chin and stared at him, amusement twinkling in her eyes. He looked at her and caught that twinkle, and for just an instant the antagonism fell away. How many times had they shared coffee and cake at his apartment or her small house while they watched that rugged TV star in action and marveled at the resemblance?

But then John's eyes went to Donald and back to Melody, and the wall was firmly in place once more.

The music began again, and Madeline let herself go, swaying to the rhythm, losing her body to it with a sensuality that made Donald gape at her. It wasn't long before she realized that Donald wasn't the only one gaping at her soft curves in their deliciously provocative cover. She danced and laughed and gave the performance of her life, while inside her something fragile and budding withered like an iced-over blossom.

A few minutes later, Melody left John to go to the ladies' room, and Donald chose that moment to go to the bar for drinks, leaving John and Madeline together as they started back through the crowd toward their respective seats.

"It won't work," he said.

"What won't?" she asked in all innocence.

"Following me around trying to explain," he said with the old, familiar arrogance. Tall, broad, sensuous, he made her want to throw herself into his arms. . . .

"I'm not following you," she said tightly.

"Then who called Josito and asked where I'd be tonight?" he growled, his silver eyes pinning hers. "Josito thought it was you."

"It was Maisie!" she countered without thinking.

"Same difference," he shot back. "Well, go ahead. Tell me he was in your bedroom as a joke."

"He was!" she bit off, her eyes unconsciously pleading with him. "It was all just to needle you!"

"It did bother me, for a minute or two," he admitted, stopping in the middle of the floor to glare down at her. "But when I came to my senses, I realized I didn't really give a damn why he was there. I don't want a woman who'll go straight from my bed to another man's."

"Then what are you doing hanging out with Melody, darling?" she asked with sweet sarcasm, unprepared for the effect the casual endearment had on him.

He caught his breath, his big body tautening as he looked at her, and for just an instant it all fell away, and they were back at the beginning, so hungry for each other that nothing else mattered. She looked into his darkening eyes, took a step toward him and stumbled clumsily.

She didn't realize that she was going down until he caught her against him and held her up.

"What is it?" he asked curtly. "Are you drunk?"

She drew in a deep, steadying breath, glorying in the feel of his hands on her, his body so close that she could feel it and smell the clean, enticing fragrance of it.

"My shoe slid," she said defiantly.

"Well, pull yourself together," he growled, his hands tightening on her bare arms, hurting. "This isn't Elise's party, and I'm not carrying you out of here in a mock faint. I told you it was over between us, and I meant it. I don't want you anymore, Madeline."

Nothing, ever, had hurt as much as those last few words. She looked up at him in an absolute fog. Her eyes, betraying the hurt, were wide and green and misty with sudden tears. Her lower lip trembled, catching his attention, and something wild shadowed over his face for an instant.

She pulled away from him, avoiding his eyes. "Excuse me, won't you?" she asked in a thin, ultrapolite tone.

"Madeline . . ." There was an uncharacteristic indecision in that deep, slow voice, but she wasn't going to wait to find out what he wanted.

She pivoted away from the table and headed into the ladies' room, darting past a stunned Melody to take refuge in one of the stalls.

When she had taken a few deep, steadying breaths, composed her features, and assured herself she was not going to cry, she joined Melody in front of the mirror. Her face was pale, and her eyes unnaturally bright.

"Something wrong?" Melody asked with a careless glance as she finished layering on red lipstick. "You don't look too great."

"Just a little too much wine," Madeline lied, closing her eyes.

Melody put away the lipstick and snapped her purse together. "Well, I'd better get back to

Johnny before he misses me. Oooh, isn't he just too much?" she sighed. "So macho... we're going to spend next weekend in Nassau—he has a house there, you know. I can hardly wait! Well, see you, honey, I hope you feel better. *Ciao!*"

The bottled up tears ran down Madeline's cheeks like raindrops. She hated John and Melody and all she wanted to do was go home and forget this terrible night.

She drew out some makeup and tried to make herself look alive. She touched up her cheeks and her mouth and went back out to the table where Donald was waiting.

He looked up as she eased into her seat, his brows drawing together.

"What the hell's the matter?" he burst out.

Her eyebrows went arching up. "What do you mean?"

"You look like a painted corpse," he replied bluntly. He grabbed the check and stood up. "We're going, right now."

"But..."

"No buts. I never should have brought you here. I'm sorry, Madeline. Come on." He put his arm around her waist and drew her along with him toward the exit. She felt John's eyes on her back, but she didn't dare look. He didn't want her anymore. She was just going to have to get used to that.

Donald saw her into the garage apartment, wavering uncertainly as he held the doorknob in his hand.

"What did he do to upset you so?" he asked, concerned.

She smiled, shaking her head. "Nothing. It was just awkward seeing him again."

He jammed his hands into his pockets, grimacing. "And my fault," he ground out. He managed to look ashamed of himself. "You're John's one weakness," he said after a minute. "Or, at least, you used to be. The only one I remember, to date. And you know what they say about love and war and fair play."

She looked up at him from her comfortable seat on the sofa bed. "Why do you hate him so?" she asked. "Surely not because your father left him those shares...."

He laughed unpleasantly, and his face hardened. For a minute, he resembled John in a bad mood. "John and I grew up together, did you know? He lived with us while his father was in the Marines. My whole life seemed to revolve around John and what he wanted. My father loved him. John could do no wrong and I could do no right.

John stayed with us until I was sixteen—just long enough to cut me completely out of my father's affection. I never measured up. Never!"

These were things she'd never known. John was usually tight-lipped about Donald and up until now Donald hadn't been forthcoming, either.

"And I could have swallowed that, all of it, without choking, even the shares being willed to John," Donald said surprisingly. "But when he married Ellen . . ."

She stared at him, finally understanding, watching his face change, soften, sadden. "You loved her," she breathed.

"I worshipped her," he corrected. "She was my girl, until John cut me out."

"He cared about her. . . ." she reminded him, recalling those rare times when John would talk about Ellen, and his life with her.

"He possessed her, totally. She couldn't breathe until she checked with John to make sure it was okay. She had no life at all unless she was in his pocket," he said bitterly. "And his life was the damned corporation. The nights she spent alone, the holidays he was out of town . . . !"

She got up to lay a gentle hand on his sleeve. "Donald, she always had the option of leaving him," she reminded him quietly. "People, for the most part, live in prisons of their own making. You can't put the responsibility for your happiness on someone else's shoulders. You have to make your own."

He sighed deeply. "Well, it doesn't matter now, does it?" he asked with a short laugh. "She's dead. And the living have to go on living, somehow. Needling John keeps me alive, you know. It gives me a reason to get up in the morning."

"What a silly reason!" she burst out.

He actually flushed. "I beg your pardon?"

"The world wasn't meant to be a morgue," she said curtly. "Ellen is dead, but you're still young and you have things to offer another woman. Why don't you stop trying to climb into her grave, and live a little? Before it's too late and you find yourself so caught up in your cruel game that you forget how to love?"

He stared down at her as if she'd hit him suddenly, his eyes blinking, glazed.

"Are you in love with John?" he asked gently.

She turned away. "He was my friend once," she hedged. "I'm very tired, Donald. Good night."

By the time the Annual Charity Ball rolled around two weeks later, Madeline's life had once again settled into a routine of hard work. She would be grateful for a little diversion, she thought as she slipped into her clinging black gown with the huge red rose on its single shoulder strap.

She'd committed herself to the ball weeks ago—before she and John had had their falling-out—and since she was on the refreshment committee, she had to be there. Donald was tied up, and couldn't go, and she was tempted to make up an excuse herself. But with a sigh she gathered her purse and went out the door. Maybe John would be out of town or unable to attend the annual affair.

When she walked through the door of the huge civic center, however, the first person she saw was John Durango.

Her knees went rubbery and she had to bite her lip to keep from crying out his name in anguish. He was wearing evening clothes, and looked so devastatingly handsome that her eyes clung to him.

He turned at that moment and looked toward her, his eyes taking in every soft curve of her body with a glitter in them that was obvious even at a distance.

She turned away, heading toward some other members of the sponsoring committee, and managed to enmesh herself in conversation before he could make a move in her direction. Not that he would have, she told herself. He'd said that it was over between them.

She managed to avoid him for most of the evening. She knew many of the people in attendance, and had partners aplenty for the graceful ballroom dances. It was a far cry from the disco, and she adored the sound of waltzes played by the live orchestra, the look of the exquisite dresses billowing as their wearers were twirled around.

It was almost midnight when Jack Rafter, a mutual friend of hers and John's, caught her hand, saying, "There you are." He dragged her over to where John was standing alone on the edge of the dance floor. "John, here's Madeline. Since you're free for this dance, and it's the last one, I can't think of a better partner for you. Go on, go on, I haven't seen you two dance together even once all night!"

Madeline wanted to hit the little man over the head with her purse, but she couldn't make a scene here, of all places. Besides, she knew he meant well.

"May I?" John asked with bitter politeness, taking her elbow to guide her onto the crowded dance floor.

The band was playing one of those lazy two-steps, a sweetly sentimental tune that made Madeline want to bolt and run. Why couldn't it have been a nice bouncy tune?

"I'm very sorry that you got landed with me," she said tautly, standing rigid as he drew her into the conventionally proper pose.

"You looked as if you'd have preferred running out the door," he replied. "But that would never have done, would it? Making a scene, God forbid!"

She flushed uncomfortably, letting her eyes go no higher than his tanned throat, above his black tie. "I come from a long line of conventional people," she reminded him.

"With the exception of your late Great-Aunt Jessie," he murmured with a reluctant smile.

She smiled stiffly. "With that exception," she murmured.

He drew in a long, harsh breath. His hand at her back spread against the silky material of the black dress. Unconsciously he drew her closer until she could feel his powerful thighs brushing against hers as they moved to the sensuous rhythm of the music.

His warm, strong hand made her tingle all over. The fingers holding her hand suddenly shifted, tangling with her fingers sensuously, easing between them in a tantalizingly slow rhythm.

His breath was coming hard now, like hers, and she felt it warm and smoky against her forehead.

"Relax against me," he whispered unsteadily, "just for a minute. Let me feel...all of you...this once."

She shouldn't have done it, but she couldn't resist him, not after the anguish she'd suffered in the weeks they'd been apart. She let her body ease against his, letting him take its full weight. His arms slid around her, supporting, clinging to every soft inch of her as his cheek slid against her temple, the mustache tickling a little when his lips touched her skin.

His fingers bit into her and she didn't even murmur, so lost was she in the pleasure of contact. Her eyes closed and her arms reached up around his neck to hold him while the music drifted around them and his thighs slid sensuously against hers through the layers of clothing.

His arms contracted as they turned and she moaned softly at the hard contact with his body, the ache, the pulsing hunger it fostered. Her face nuzzled into his warm throat and she drank in the woodsy smell of his cologne. "John..." she whispered achingly.

"Closer?" he whispered. "Like this?" He shifted his arms, lowering them, pressing her body into intimate contact with his, and she felt a sudden tremor in his big arms.

She caught her breath, her face contorting in anguish as she clung. "Oh, don't," she whispered miserably, "please don't, I can't...bear it!"

"You still want me," he growled. "I can feel it."

"No!" She drew away from him, her eyes burning with unshed tears as she looked up into his fiery eyes. "It's all over, you said so." A single tear escaped from her eye and rolled down her flushed cheek as she remembered. "You said ... you didn't want me anymore."

She jerked away from him, turning to walk quickly off the dance floor. He caught up with her as she made it to the door and started out into the night, his arm sliding around her smoothly to draw her into the shadows near one of the tall pillars at the front entrance.

"Not yet, you don't," he growled, holding her against him. "You're driving me out of my mind!"

"Wrong girl," she pointed out, wiping angrily at the tears. "Haven't you forgotten your little blond friend?"

He drew an angry breath, shaking her gently. "Forget Melody!"

"But John, she's so sweet, so willing, so *young!*" she reminded him, struggling against the crush of his body.

"Stop that," he said in an odd, taut voice, catching her hips to hold her still.

She leaned her head back to see his strained, hard face. "What's the matter, John, do I disturb you?" she laughed bitterly.

"My God, what a question," he ground out. His eyes were frightening. He studied her face quietly for a long time. "Tell me what my cousin was doing in your room that night."

She blinked. "I beg your pardon?"

He lifted his head, staring down at her. "I'm willing to listen to an explanation, if you have one."

"Why, John, how generous of you!" she exclaimed. "What a pity that I've decided I don't owe you one."

His hands on her hips tightened. "You're as hungry for me as I am for you," he ground out, bending. "And you'll tell me what I want to know . . . one way or another."

His mouth crushed down against hers, and it was all of heaven. Try as she would, she couldn't stand in his embrace and pretend to be calm. Her heart threatened to burst, her lungs seemed incapable of keeping up with the demand on them. Her nails bit into the fine cloth of his jacket, her mouth opening to his, her body trembling, and a long, sweet moan came from her throat.

"Oh, God, I need you," he whispered into her mouth, nipping at it with his teeth, tracing it with his tongue before he took it, roughly, again. "I need you!"

She would have said the same thing, but her voice had long since deserted her. She locked her arms around him and yielded without a protest, letting him take what he wanted, giving back everything she had in the way of response.

His mouth slid against her cheek finally, down into the soft waves at her ear, the harshness of his breathing and the heavy throb of his heartbeat telling her without words that he was as affected as she was.

"Come home with me, Madeline," he whispered gruffly, and a shudder of unbearable need went through his big body. His arms tightened, emphasizing the emotion in his voice as he let her feel the aching tautness of his body.

She gathered herself together, and pushed gently against his chest. Surprisingly, he let her go without a protest.

She turned away, clutching her purse, and tried to steady her breath. "No, John," she said quietly.

"Is he that good?" he growled harshly.

She whirled, her face flaming at the insult, missing the frustrated pain in his eyes as she met his regard. "Damn you!" she threw at him.

"Temper, temper," he chided, eyeing her sparkling green eyes and wild hair with masculine appreciation. "God, you're pretty when you want to bite!"

"I'd like to bite you!" she ground out.

He moved a step closer. "Come home with me, and I'll let you." His voice dropped caressingly. "You bit me that night, remember, Madeline?" he murmured.

She did, and she flushed red. Before she could think up a good retort, he was so close she couldn't think at all. Her heart pounded furiously and she knew she wanted to go with him. But she didn't dare, not now....

"Come home with me," he murmured. "You know you want to."

She drew in a shaky breath and turned her face away. "I'll admit that I owe you a lot," she whispered, "for teaching me how to appreciate my body. But I really can't leave Donald alone any longer. He's waiting up for me." She pulled away, but she couldn't look at him after telling the blatant lie. Only by lying would she escape his bed.

He went rigid; his eyes faded to ice. "Don't let me keep you, then," he said curtly. "After all, honey, one body's as good as another."

She whirled on rubbery legs and walked quickly toward her car. Thank goodness she'd managed to get away before she gave in to him. Loving him, wanting him, she would have gone to the end of the world if he'd asked her to. And she couldn't let that happen, not when he thought she was a tramp already. She couldn't reinforce his opinion that she was . . . easy.

Tears were rolling freely down her cheeks as she locked the car and started it. Life was beginning to be unbearable without John.

Chapter Eight

She lay awake for hours, agonizing over the lie she'd told John. In all their time together, she couldn't remember ever lying to him before. Whatever he thought of her, even if he understood her vulnerability, she had to tell him she hadn't gone home to Donald's bed.

She reached for the receiver and lifted it. After all, what did she have to lose? Only her pride, her self-respect . . .

The phone rang and rang, and her fingers trembled on the receiver. It was past midnight, but surely he hadn't gone to bed already. Not John, who was a night owl of the first order. Her heart beat wildly in her chest. Had he been as miserable as she? The way he'd reacted to her at the charity ball had proved one thing, that he still wanted her. Perhaps there was still time to patch things up, before the chasm between them got any wider.

Finally the receiver at the other end was lifted. "Durango residence." It was Josito's voice, stiff and troubled.

"Hello, Josito, it's me," she said hesitantly.

There was a short pause. "It . . . it is good to hear your voice, *señorita,*" he said, his tone stilted. "May I be of service?"

"May I speak to John?" she asked quickly, before she could change her mind.

Josito cleared his throat. *"Momentito,"* he murmured. "Uh, Señor Durango, it is Miss Vigny. . . ."

There was a pause and a burst of profanity, followed by staccato commands too sharp and muffled to be understood. Madeline felt her heart stop in her chest as she waited.

Josito cleared his throat again. "Uh, *señorita,*" he began, his voice rigid, "he say . . ."

"Tell her, damn you!" she heard John bellow from nearby.

"I am sorry, *señorita,*" Josito continued in a slow, pained voice, "but he say he does not want to speak with you and he . . . he say . . ."

"Will you tell her, damn you!" John ground out over Josito's voice.

Josito took a deep breath. "He say...he never want...to see you or speak with you...again, and not to...to bother him anymore."

Her eyes closed. She didn't even try to answer. She laid the phone gently back in the cradle and tears bled down her cheeks, into her mouth. She'd never been one to cry, not unless it was something momentous—but then, this was. This was as close to mourning for a living person as she'd ever come. It was as if John had just declared her dead, and was burying her alive. Because without him, that was what life was going to amount to.

The rest of the weekend went by in a painful haze. Then, Monday morning brought a glimmer of pleasure. Bill Gonnells called to tell Madeline that her house was ready to be occupied.

She started evacuating the garage apartment immediately, tossing clothes into little heaps into the back of the yellow VW while Donald watched, his hands in his pockets, his eyes wistful. He'd been different lately—more relaxed, happier.

"I've enjoyed having you here," he said with a smile. "And not just because it annoyed John."

She smiled back. "I've enjoyed being here. That's a favor I owe you."

His eyebrows went up. "You mean, if my roof ever caves in, you'll let me stay in the tree house out behind your house?"

"It doesn't have a roof, or walls," she pointed out.

His chin lifted. "I was a Boy Scout!"

She shrugged. "Then, it's yours in an emergency. Donald, I really do appreciate the loan of the apartment," she added seriously.

"It was my pleasure." He eyed her closely. "You're awfully pale these days. Maybe you ought to see a doctor...."

She turned away. "I'm just living on nerves, that's all," she said doggedly. "Besides, I can't be sick, I'm gaining weight." She tugged at the waistband of her slacks. They were unbuttoned because she couldn't make the button and buttonhole stay together.

"You still worry me."

"How kind," she murmured, batting her long eyelashes at him. "Now, you will forward any phone calls?" she asked.

He eyed her closely. "From John, you mean?"

She flushed. "From anybody."

"Of course." He cleared his throat. "Uh, would you like me to tell him the truth about that night with the champagne?"

"No," she said. "Because then I'd have to tell him the truth about the charity ball—I sort of let him think that you were waiting up for me," she confessed.

His eyebrows arched. "Why?"

She grimaced. "That's a long story. It did the trick very well, unfortunately. And when I tried to call him back and tell him the truth, he wouldn't talk to me. He said for me not to ever 'bother' him again."

"Maybe he was just out of sorts and didn't mean it," Donald suggested. "He does have a nasty temper."

"Maybe," she sighed. "I'll just have to wait and see."

It didn't take long. Late that afternoon, the Rolls purred to a stop in her driveway. She watched out the window, heart racing, only to be swamped with disappointment when she realized that it was Josito, not John. He was carrying a small box, and he looked like doomsday.

She opened the door before he could ring the bell. "Well?" she asked hopefully. Maybe it was a peace offering.

He placed the cardboard box in her hands. In it were little odds and ends that she'd left at John's house over the years, including some snapshots he'd taken of her during that time. She wanted to cry as she stared down at the memorabilia.

"I am sorry," Josito groaned. "He is like a wounded animal, I cannot even speak with him. What he made me say to you on the phone...I am so sorry, *señorita,* but he would not even let me call and apologize, he said he would fire me. And he meant it."

"Fire you?" she gasped. "But you've been with him for..."

"*Sí,* that is so," Josito agreed. He shrugged his shoulders, looking just a bit taller in the dark suit he was wearing. "But he has no qualms about firing people these days. He was always a stern man, but lately he is hard like a brick wall. The night you called, he took a bottle of whiskey to his room and could not lift his head yesterday morning. It is the first time since Mrs. Durango died that I have known him to drink like that." He shook his head. "When he had sobered up, he made me go through the house and find every single thing of yours and bring it here—that is, to Señor Donald's house. He told me that you had left.'' He sighed. ''What can I say?'' he asked, spreading his hands. ''He flings mashed potatoes on his plate because they are too creamy, he makes me say terrible things to his old friend, you, on the phone. But last week he did the strangest thing—that TV show he watched with you all the time? It came on and he picked up that big pot of African violets on the coffee table and smashed the TV screen with it!''

She lowered her eyes to the box, although she could barely see it anymore.

''He's really had it with me, hasn't he, Josito?'' she asked in a painful, husky voice. She laughed softly. ''It's my own fault, I suppose. I lied to him. . . .'' She shook her head to clear her vision. ''You'd better get back while you still have a job, and I've got work to do, too. Thanks, anyway, Josito.''

''Sí, señorita. Lo siento mucho . . .''

''I'm sorry, too, old friend,'' she said gently. ''Josito, take care of him. He pushes himself so hard.''

He nodded. ''I will always do that. Even though,'' he added darkly, ''at this moment it would give me such great pleasure to back one of his cars over him two or three times.''

"Shame on you," she chided. "You know how expensive tires are!''

He sighed. "You do have a point.''

"Josito..." She avoided his eyes. "Is he, uh, still seeing Melody? She mentioned one night that he was taking her to Nassau for a weekend.''

"Melody?" He frowned. "*Señorita*, he has spent most of his nights at the office working himself into an early grave. And when he was not there, he was causing his cowboys to start attending church services.''

Her eyebrows arched. "Preaching to them...?''

"Oh, no, *señorita*, they go to church to pray to God to deliver them from him," he replied solemnly. *"Adios, señorita."*

The next morning she couldn't lift her head for a bout of nausea that all but knocked her to her knees. Overreaction, she convinced herself, just emotional shock from John's treatment of her.

But as the days turned into weeks and the nausea didn't improve, she began to worry. Perhaps it was overwork. She got into bed and stayed there for two days, surprised when Donald showed up one morning with a small canvas under his arm.

She answered the door in her burgundy velour robe, her hair wild, her face pale.

"Hi," she said weakly.

He gaped at her, his face expressive. "My God, what's the matter with you?" he burst out.

"Just a virus," she promised him. "What's that?" she added, nodding toward his package.

He held up a painting of her small house with the little VW parked beside it, and grinned. "Housewarming present," he murmured. "I thought it might cheer you up."

She hated the tears that rushed to her eyes. She'd been horribly emotional lately, so much so that she'd stopped watching sentimental old movies on TV. "Oh, thank you. How very thoughtful, Donald!"

He shrugged, looking uncomfortable. "I didn't have anything better to do...." He eyed her up and down. "Seen John lately?" he asked quietly.

She shook her head with a pale smile. "That's all over, you know."

He grimaced. "Think you'll ever forgive me?" he asked.

She touched his arm gently. "It would have happened eventually, anyway," she assured him. "Donald, I really have to lie down again," she added with a smile. "I'm pretty sick."

"Can I get you anything?" he asked. "Want me to call the doctor?"

She shook her head. "It's just one of those nagging things that comes and goes," she said vaguely. "But it's sure the devil to get rid of. It's sapping my energy. I've had to take the typewriter to bed with me," she sighed.

"Well, if you need anything, call me, okay?" he asked.

"You're a love, Donald. Thank you."

He nodded, making a helpless gesture as he turned and went down the steps.

She turned back into the house and closed the door. If only she could get back on her feet, she groaned silently. Perhaps she just needed to push herself a little harder. It could be just laziness, or emotional depression. She'd spend one more day in bed, and then she'd get up and get back to work.

She got on with the book, but finally she was forced to recognize that this was something other than a virus. And she had a strong suspicion that she knew what it was. She and John hadn't bothered with precautions that wild night they spent together, and for two weeks she'd been afraid of seeing a doctor because the symptoms had been almost definite. Now it was six weeks since she'd been with John, and she went to the doctor's office with a cold, deathly fear in her heart.

He had her go to the lab for tests, his friendly, kind attitude telling her nothing. The next morning, she called his office for the results and absorbed the shock. She was pregnant.

Pregnant! She wandered around in a numb trance for the next half hour. One phone call, and her whole life had been turned upside down.

She walked into the living room and sat down in her big easy chair, her hands going involuntarily to her growing waistline. All of a sudden, she was aware of life inside her body. Of a tiny blossoming bud. A child.

She stared blankly at the new white curtains she'd just hung, and thought absently how pretty they looked and what a good thing it was that she'd had them packed away in the bedroom closet. Then she laughed at her own mundane musings. She was sitting there, unmarried, pregnant, alone in the world, and all she could think about was new curtains.

With a sigh, she leaned back against the cushions. Well, at least she knew now what was causing the nausea and faintness that had plagued her. Some virus!

A baby. She smiled to herself, thinking about little lacy things and someone to love, protect and take care of. A sweet-smelling, soft little child that would grow up...

She caught her breath. Now, that was a thought. What kind of future would a fatherless child have? Houston was no small town, but she was well known in it. She wasn't going to be able to stay here. It wouldn't be fair to the baby to let the stigma of illegitimacy be attached to it. Of course, she could go and propose marriage to Donald, she had a feeling he'd marry her in a minute—but that would hardly be fair. And if John found out she was pregnant... She laughed bitterly. He'd think it was Donald's, that was what he'd think. He and Ellen hadn't been able to have children, and she knew for a fact that John had always refused to have any tests done to find out whose fault that was. He had every reason in the world to believe he was sterile.

For just an instant she entertained the thought of telling him—but only for an instant. If he wouldn't believe the truth about Donald, he certainly wasn't going to believe that this child was his. And, too, she hadn't the heart for another battle with him. He could hurt her too much. That was the problem with having friends turn into enemies: they knew where to hit and wound the most.

After a while, when the numbness and shock wore off, she made herself a cup of tea and started thinking about what she could do, where she could go. She had a maiden aunt in Georgia, in a little community outside Atlanta. If she invented a husband tragically killed . . .

She finished her tea and set the cup aside. Strangely, she found herself looking forward to the months of pregnancy. It didn't occur to her to feel trapped by the impending certainty of motherhood, or to resent her baby. She smiled, thinking how nice it would be to have someone else around the house. Perhaps a little boy who'd look like his father; she could give him all the love that John Durango didn't want. She'd name him Cameron, if he was a boy, she decided immediately. It was John's middle name, and she liked the sound of it. And Edward, for her late father. Cameron Edward . . . Vigny. No, she couldn't use her own maiden name, she'd have to invent one. She frowned. Well, time enough for that later. Right now, there was a chapter to start typing into manuscript.

She got up from the chair and started toward her desk when the doorbell rang. Oh, no, she thought, please don't let it be Miss Rose with another hour of ferocious conversation about the noisy neighbors across the street.

She opened the door, expecting Miss Rose. What she found was John Durango, with a bouquet of dark red roses in one hand.

Chapter Nine

She stared up at him in shock, her body reacting as if she'd found the French Navy outside her door. Her mind automatically registered how handsome he looked in his blue blazer and white trousers with a white silk shirt open at the neck, and a creamy white Stetson atop his crisply waving hair.

"I had a long talk with my cousin," he said after a minute, his face hard, his eyes narrowed and appraising as they studied her face. "He was right, you don't look well at all."

She felt herself stiffen. *Now* he decided to make up, when it was too late for them to have anything together; when she was pregnant and didn't dare tell him for fear that he'd marry her out of a

sense of obligation. Because he didn't love her—
he couldn't after the way he'd treated her. Bitterness gathered in her throat, choking her.

"How nice of you to drop by, but the housewarming won't be until 1995. I'll be sure you get
an invitation," she added pleasantly, trying to
close the door.

He got his shiny boot between it and the door
jamb and stopped her from closing it.

"Aren't you going to ask me in, even for old
time's sake?" he asked quietly, searching her face,
her eyes, as if he was starving to death for the
sight of her.

"No, I'm not," she replied calmly. "Your foot
seems to be in the way. Could you move it
please?"

He grimaced, the mustache lifting and falling
impatiently. "I didn't mean what I had Josito tell
you," he said after a minute, in a curt, angered
tone. He hated apologies, he never made them—
this was as close as he was going to come, too.

"Didn't you?" she asked, looking up at him
for a moment with a world of sadness in her eyes.

His big hand contracted around the green pa-
per that framed the dark red roses. "My God,
what did you expect me to do, crawl on my

knees—after you'd told me you were going straight from me to my cousin's bed!''

"You might have believed in me," she replied, her green eyes accusing. "From the very beginning, when you found me in the garage apartment, you thought the worst. You thought that I couldn't wait to jump into bed with Donald. And that's what I can't forgive, John, that you didn't trust me!"

"You don't understand how it's been between my cousin and me," he ground out. "Not just recently, but for years now, and especially since Ellen died. He's hated me for things I couldn't help, that I had no control over. Neither one of us made any effort to straighten it all out, until this morning. He . . . told Josito he wanted to talk to me. I had him come over to the office, and we talked—about the past, and about you." He drew in a deep, harsh breath. "He was worried about the way you look."

"I'm just on my way in a few minutes to buy some more clothes and have my hair done," she assured him.

"Not that!" he growled. "The way you look— pale as a ghost and—" he scowled "—different."

Watch it, old girl, she schooled herself, don't give the apples away. She tossed back her long, waving red gold hair, watching the way his eyes clung to it.

"I'm working against a deadline, and I haven't had a lot of sleep," she said quietly. "But I went to the doctor yesterday, and he says I'm in great shape."

For a pregnant lady, she added silently.

He relaxed a little, but the frown still held his heavy brows together. "Are you sure he knew what he was doing?" he asked hesitantly.

"You must think so, you send your men to him," she shot back. "Now, John, I'm very busy...."

"So am I, dammit, I'm supposed to be in a meeting with some sheik from Saudi Arabia right now about an oil lease!"

"Then don't let me keep you," she replied, trying again to close the door.

He looked as if he wanted to chew something—like tenpenny nails. "Will you listen!"

"Sure," she replied. "The same way you listened when I tried to explain about Donald."

"He told me all about that," he said bitterly, "about what he said, and why. And about what you said to me at the charity ball," he added, his eyes almost pleading—as if those silver fires could plead.

She flushed wildly, averting her eyes. "That's all over now," she said firmly, aching miserably inside. "It's past history. Let's just . . . let it go."

"I can't," he said in a harsh note. "Don't you understand that I can't?"

She turned glaring at him. "What did Donald tell you?" she asked, studying the pained look on his face. Was there any guilt mixed in, was that what caused that look in his eyes? He couldn't possibly know about the baby, there was simply no way. So what was it?

"Will you at least take the roses?" he asked with cold dignity. "The damned things are giving me hay fever."

"Certainly!" she replied. She took the roses from his hand and proceeded slowly and deliberately to crush the deep red heads against the front of his silk shirt.

She got up the next morning, took one of the nausea tablets the doctor had prescribed, and dressed in a loose blouse and a pair of unbuttoned slacks. She needed some looser clothes and that was going to be the first order of business today.

She wouldn't buy maternity clothes. Not yet, not until she decided what cock-and-bull story she was going to hand her sweet but fluffy-minded aunt when she asked if she could come and live with her. What a blessing that she was successful enough not to have to hold down a daily job. Finances were the least of her worries.

She wanted some slacks with elastic waistbands, but amazingly enough she couldn't find any. In desperation she went to the shopping mall near John's office, hoping she wouldn't run into him. That confrontation yesterday had nearly finished her; it had taken the better part of an hour for her to calm down.

In a small boutique, she found just what she was looking for. She bought four pairs of light-colored slacks two sizes larger than she usually wore, and two pretty, loose blouses to match them. Afterward, she went out onto the mall to sit down and catch her breath. She was so hot that she could barely breathe at all, and she was feeling sicker by the minute. She dropped her purse on purpose to give her an excuse to lower her head, hoping the faintness and nausea would pass. But they didn't. It was only half a block or so to her car, but it might as well have been six miles for all the good that did her.

She would have given half a book's royalties just for some ice or a wet cloth. Glancing around, she saw that all the nearby shops were dry goods places—not one of them a snack bar. Fate, she thought with bitter humor.

After a minute, she decided to try walking anyway. There was nothing else she could do except make the effort, or sit there all day.

Clutching her purse and the package, she got up from the bench and started in the direction of the mall exit. The walls seemed to swing crazily toward her, and the people began to blur. She saw a big, imposing man in a dark suit and a Stetson coming toward her, but his face didn't register. Everything went a startling silver and black, and she felt herself crumpling. . . .

She came to lying on a plush sofa, a totally alien ceiling swimming into focus above her head. She closed her eyes again, blinked, and took a deep breath. At least, thank goodness, the nausea had passed. She felt calm and quiet and not at all sick or faint. Her head turned, and she looked straight into John Durango's fiercely worried eyes.

"Feeling better?" he asked with a cold smile.

She looked around. There were three strange men staring at her from the doorway while John sat beside her on the couch.

"Much, thank you," she managed in a strained voice.

"Then would you mind telling me what the hell you were doing walking all over creation in this kind of heat and fainting in the mall?" he demanded curtly.

She glared at him, pulling herself into a sitting position. "I'm buying clothes, what does it look like?" she lashed out at him, pointing to the bag lying on the nearby coffee table. "And what business is it of yours where I faint? Do you own the mall?"

The men in the doorway were discreetly retreating, one pausing to close the door behind him.

"Would you like something cold to drink?" he asked after a minute, his concern getting the best of his temper. His eyes slid over her body, as if he was looking for a wound that might have brought her down. They were too well concealed beneath his lids for her to see the expression in them.

"I could do with a small Coke," she admitted. The air-conditioning in the office felt good to her overheated skin.

"I'll get you one." He moved away, leaving her to look at her surroundings and get her wits back. It was a nice office, done in blues and grays, with plush furniture and a beautifully polished wood desk. Whoever had decorated it had good taste.

Only a minute later, John was back with a frosted can of Coke. He handed it to her, opened.

She took a long sip and smiled. "You're a magician," she murmured.

"I'm very definitely that," he murmured with a strange, faint smile on his chiseled lips, a light in his steely eyes that was puzzling, exciting.

She ignored him, sipping the cold liquid until she felt sure that she wasn't going to get sick or faint again.

"How about something to eat?" he asked. "What have you had today?"

"Some tea," she murmured sheepishly.

"Idiot," he grumbled, but there was the old tender concern in his voice. "Come on. I'll buy you lunch."

"It isn't time," she protested.

"I'll buy you breakfast."

"It's past eleven."

He cocked an eyebrow down at her. "Honey, if I want breakfast at midnight, I can get it. Would you like to make a bet?"

She smiled. It was the first time she'd smiled at him in ages. The effect it had on John was fascinating. He stared at her for so long that she dropped her eyes in shy confusion, her heart running wild.

"Coming, Satin?" he asked gently.

She reached down to get her purse and purchases, her heart rejoicing at the sound of the nickname. It was good to know that he wasn't angry anymore. Even though she didn't dare let things progress to the point they had before, perhaps they could be friends again . . . at least until she moved away. That would be a little bit of heaven to take with her.

They had bacon and eggs at one of the restaurants on the mall, astonishing the early lunch crowd.

"I know the chef," he murmured, his mustache curling under a grin as he polished off the last piece of toast and sat back to sip his coffee.

"I'm glad you do," she sighed, stuffed. "I can't remember being so hungry."

He chuckled, his face relaxed, his eyes faintly amused, tender as they swept over her. "Have enough?"

"More than enough, thanks." She smiled, glancing at the empty plate.

"Eggs are good for you if you're prone to fainting. Lots of protein. Steak isn't bad, either." He cocked his head. "How about one tonight?"

She stiffened, her eyes wary as they met his, the fear in them evident. "I don't know...."

He leaned forward, his face quiet, caring. "Honey, I won't try to take you to bed again," he said softly. "I promise you that. I won't even touch you if you don't want me to."

She stared at him, fascinated. "Can we go back?" she asked involuntarily.

"No," he admitted. "Only forward. One step at a time, one day at a time. No commitments, no strings, on either side. No dragging up the past."

Her eyes lovingly traced every craggy line of his face. She shouldn't accept. If she had any sense, she'd get up and run. But she loved him too much to refuse these few little crumbs of comfort from him. A few more days in his company couldn't hurt. All too soon, her condition would become obvious and she'd have to leave Houston. But right now, she only looked well-fed. He wouldn't even suspect. If she could stop fainting, that was. But an empty stomach might have caused that, and he was a man. What did he know about pregnant women?

"All right," she said after a minute.

He brightened. "I'll have Josito come after you about six. Better yet, we'll both come."

Her eyes widened. "My goodness, I don't need an armed escort!"

He shifted uncomfortably and looked away. "I don't want you driving around alone at night. Humor me, will you?"

"But I've always done it before," she protested.

He looked as if he was dying to say something, but couldn't. The mustache twitched irritably. "There have been two robberies in one week on your street. At night. Late. Just humor me, will you, dammit?"

She laughed at the controlled ferocity in his face. "All right. It's your gas."

"Damned straight, it's my gas," he replied. "What good is owning an oil company if you can't enjoy using your own product?"

She couldn't argue with that.

The Rolls purred up the driveway at six sharp, with Josito grinning at the wheel and John looking like a fashion plate in his dark evening clothes as he climbed out of the back seat to help her inside.

His eyes approved of the long, black gown—it was the same one she'd worn to the charity ball, but she'd changed the red rose for a white one. She hadn't had much choice about which dress to wear: this was the only one in the closet that would still fit.

"Where are we going?" she asked curiously.

"To where they serve the best steak in Houston," he replied with a smile.

"And where is that?"

"My apartment."

She felt her cheeks going white as she stared at him. His hand came out and caught hers in a warm, reassuring grasp. It was warm and faintly rough against her smooth skin, and the touch of it made music in her blood.

"There's nothing to be afraid of," he said quietly. "I meant what I told you earlier. And Josito's going to be there all night. He'll protect you with his very life."

She relaxed. But only a little. The memories were going to come rushing back the minute she walked through the door, and she was afraid of them.

Her eyes scanned John's rugged face. What would he do, she wondered, if she looked him in the eye and said, "John, I'm pregnant?" A tiny mischievous smile flared in her eyes and died before she lifted them. He'd probably faint, she thought. After which... She didn't dare think about afterward. Her fingers clutched her purse firmly. She had to control herself.

"Okay," she said. "Where did the steak come from? The ranch?"

He gaped at her with an appalled expression. "The ranch? My God, I don't run beef cattle!"

She blinked. "I thought we were friends."

"We are."

"Is one of those pedigreed, mangy old cows of yours too good to serve your friend?" she prodded.

He shifted impatiently. "Those 'mangy old cows' bring around twenty-five thousand dollars or more at auction. They're purebred. You don't eat purebred breeding cattle."

"Why not? Do you have to eat the papers with them?"

He drew in a slow breath. "God give me patience..."

"He did not," she pointed out. "You have absolutely no patience."

"I did once," he reminded her with a slow, tender smile.

She blushed to the roots of her hair and caught her breath, avoiding his penetrating gaze.

There was a short pause before he asked, quietly, "Are you still ashamed of what happened?"

Now there was a question. She looked out the window at the beautiful night lights of the city. "Isn't Houston pretty at night?" she asked with forced brightness.

He only laughed, and it sounded vaguely predatory.

The steak was incredibly tender. Josito served it with homemade rolls, baked potatoes smothered in sour cream and a cold, crisp salad. There was a peach cobbler for dessert. Madeline ate as if it were going to be her last meal, aware of John's amused gaze the whole time.

"Well, it was delicious," she said defensively, her lower lip thrusting out at him.

"I'm glad you enjoyed it," he replied. He got up, holding her chair for her, and led her into the living room.

"Brandy?" he asked.

She almost accepted it, then changed her mind. Alcohol wouldn't be good for the baby.

He smiled as he went to pour himself a small whiskey, eyeing her over the rim of the glass.

"Rather have whiskey?" he chided, and laughed when she made a horrible face.

He leaned back against the bar and stood just looking at her, his silvery eyes glancing over every rounded inch of her body with a purely possessive boldness.

She lifted her chin. "Looking for rips in the material?" she asked politely.

He shook his head, still smiling. "It becomes you, honey," he said in a deep, hushed tone.

Her eyes immediately became suspicious. "What does?"

"Gaining weight, of course. I've noticed, you know," he muttered as he raised the glass to his lips and sipped the amber liquid. "What did you think I meant?"

She flushed, looking away. "Nothing."

He laughed softly as he moved to sit down beside her on the plush couch. She glanced at him warily, remembering the last time they'd shared this sofa, and what it had led to.

"Don't look so threatened," he murmured gently. "I promised not to touch you, didn't I?"

"You do it very well with your eyes, John Durango," she informed him. He was very close, and she felt the impact of that closeness—the warmth of him, the clean, male scent of his cologne. She crossed her legs and tightened the clasp of her fingers in her lap.

He sighed deeply, leaning back. His eyes closed, and he looked as if he'd just returned from months in the desert.

"Tired?" she asked with involuntary concern.

His mouth smiled under the bushy mustache. "Dead. I've kept up a killing work schedule." One eye opened, watching her. "Not to mention being out of sorts with you."

She flushed. "Don't put all the blame on me, if you please," she bristled. "It was your suspicious mind that started the whole thing."

He shook his head. "No, honey, it was taking you to bed that started it." He caught her eyes, his head turning sideways against the back of the sofa, and there was an expression in them that made her tingle all over. "Was it as rough on you as it was on me, having a sword between us?"

She nodded. "We've been very close over the years, and I didn't realize how much time we spent together until we weren't doing it anymore." She smiled wistfully. "I . . . felt alone."

"So did I." He caught her fingers in his big, warm ones and held them gently. "Madeline, suppose we . . . spent a lot more time together."

"How do you mean?"

He took a deep breath and looked straight into her curious eyes. "I mean, why don't we get married?"

She felt the shock of the words right down to her toes. She froze, staring at him as though she'd gone mute.

He grimaced. "Damn, I shouldn't have sprung it on you like that. I meant to lead up to it . . . well, it's too late now," he said stubbornly, his jaw tightening. "Will you?"

Her lips tried to make words, trembled, and tried again. "We . . . you said you'd never marry again," she faltered.

"So I changed my mind," he growled. He fumbled in his pocket for a cigarette and retrieved his gold-plated lighter from his pocket.

She watched him light the cigarette, startled at the suddenness of his proposal. He said he wanted to marry her, yet he had never spoken of love. If he loved her, how could he have treated her the way he had the past six weeks? It didn't make sense, none of it made sense. And then there was the baby. . . .

If only she could trust him not to hurt her the way he had before. But if he had reacted so violently to the mere sight of Donald in her bedroom, how would he react to the news that she was pregnant? Would she ever be able to convince him that the child was his, not Donald's? She didn't think she could bear the hurt of having him turn away from her again. She wished she had the time to be sure of his feelings, to build up his trust in her. But time was one thing she didn't have. In another month or so her pregnancy would begin to show.... Oh, God, it was an impossible situation.

"I can't marry you," she said at last.

He studied her quietly, smiling at the fear and uncertainty he read in her lovely face. "Oh, I think you will," he murmured. "All you need is a chance to get used to the idea. I always get my way, honey, and I happen to want you like hell." His voice lowered, softened. "Now more than ever."

That light in his eyes puzzled her.

"Why?" she demanded.

His darkening eyes slid down every taut inch of her body in the clinging black dress, and he smiled wickedly. "You'd be shocked at the reasons," he murmured. "Come here and I'll show you a few of them."

She grabbed up her purse from the coffee table and walked deliberately toward the door. "Goodbye, John," she ground out. "Thanks for the steak."

"How were you planning to get home?" he asked politely.

She paused with her hand on the doorknob, thinking. "I'll get a cab."

He chuckled. "Wait a minute. I'll have Josito run you over to the house. And this time I won't insist on going along. Does that brighten your evening?"

"Yes," she said defiantly.

But he only smiled, getting up from the sofa like a big, graceful cat. "Just remember, Satin. You'll see it my way sooner or later."

The house was beginning to look like a florist's shop. Every day there was another dozen roses—red ones, pink ones, white ones, apricot ones—from John.

If he wasn't sending flowers, he was calling. Or having food delivered—he knew she wouldn't make herself breakfast, so he had Josito run over with hot plates of bacon, eggs and homemade biscuits every morning. And she found out the first day that if she didn't eat them, he'd simply keep sending the poor little man back with more until she did. For Josito's sake, she cleared the plate.

But she wouldn't talk to him, despite the fact that he phoned six times a day, at regular intervals. She was afraid to talk to him, she admitted to herself. John could bulldoze a brick wall, he was so persuasive, but this was one decision she had to make on her own. She needed to think, and she couldn't do that with John around. For once in his life John Durango was going to learn that he couldn't always get his way through sheer force of will.

She went to the grocery store Friday afternoon, as was her habit, parking in her usual spot. But she'd no sooner gotten out of the car than she was aware of being watched.

She stopped in front of a bake-sale table outside the store entrance as John Durango came striding up on the sidewalk, wearing a blue pin-striped suit, his familiar white Stetson, and a furious black scowl.

"Why in hell won't you talk to me?" he growled. "Don't you like the damned roses?"

"I have to like them," she countered angrily, "they've covered up two rooms. I'm using them to stuff pillows, to flavor soups, to decorate cakes.... I'm even bathing in the damned things!''

"I thought you liked roses."

"I do, but I didn't want to be buried in them!" she wailed. "I've long ago run out of vases. All my cooking pots are now full of roses—I'll starve!"

He brightened. "I'll have Josito bring over lunch and supper, too."

"No!" she burst out, aware of the curious, amused looks they were getting from the three bake-sale ladies. "Breakfast is enough, thank you. I can manage the rest. You know I hate breakfast," she added accusingly.

"You've been ill," he replied stubbornly, his lower lip jutting out. "You need to get your strength back." He grinned. "If you'd marry me, I could fatten you up. I could spoon-feed you your meals."

"I am not, repeat *not,* going to marry you!" she burst out in exasperation. "Please, John. Just go away!"

"Not until you say yes," he replied. He stuck his hands in his pockets. "I've got all day free. I'll just tag along with you."

"In that case, you're going to get pretty hungry, aren't you?" she asked, her lips pursing thoughtfully.

He shrugged. "I'll get a bite to eat somewhere along the way."

"Oh, allow me to take care of that little problem for you." She turned, studying the array of foodstuffs. "Lemon meringue," she said to John, picking up a pie. "Your favorite, isn't it?"

He nodded. "As a matter of fact, it is."

Holding the pie in one hand, she dug out a five dollar bill and handed it to one of the ladies at the table with a nice smile.

"Here, darling," she told John, batting her eyelashes at him. "Enjoy it."

And she reached up and smashed it in the middle of his face.

She'd thought the pie would discourage him. But the next morning when she went out to jog down the street, hoping it would get her started after a sleepless night, the sound of a car caught her ear.

She moved over to the side of the road to let it pass, idly wondering why anyone sane would be up at this ungodly hour—besides crazy pregnant women who couldn't seem to sit still, that was.

But when several seconds went by and the car still didn't pass, she looked over her shoulder.

There, behind her, keeping pace with her graceful movements, was the white Rolls, Josito at the wheel and John leaning out the open back window, grinning at her through his neatly trimmed black mustache.

Chapter Ten

"Good morning," John said.

"Good morning," she returned curtly, ignoring him as she continued to jog. She counted her steps: one, two, three, four, five, six, seven. . . .

"Nice weather we're having," he persisted, gazing up through the thick green leaves on the hardwood trees that lined the street. "For early summer, that is."

"Very nice," she panted. She forced herself not to look at him.

"Why don't you take a breather and ride along with us?" John invited after a minute.

She glared at him. "Why don't you get out of that car and take a little exercise? Didn't you used to say that executives who sat at desks went to seed?''

There was a pause, the sound of a door opening and closing, and a minute later John was jogging along beside her with Josito pacing them in the luxurious car.

Even in worn jeans and a yellow knit shirt, he looked elegant, she thought, approving of his big, muscular body against her will as he trotted lazily alongside her.

''You really look like him this morning,'' she murmured.

''Like whom?''

''That guy on TV,'' she teased. ''Except that he wears sneakers, not boots.''

He grinned, one side of the mustache lifting. ''In the series, he couldn't afford boots.''

''I reckon not, partner,'' she drawled.

He glanced at her. ''Thanks for the pie, by the way. What I tasted of it was delicious.''

''You're very welcome.'' She burst out laughing. ''I'm sorry, really I am, it just seemed the thing to do at the time.''

''Like lobbing that plate of spaghetti into my lap?'' he mused.

''I thought you liked spaghetti!''

"I used to," he agreed. He glanced at her. "You're damned pale. Feel okay?"

"Sure," she lied. Actually, she was feeling pretty green. But she was determined not to let it show. She started counting mentally again.

"Do you have any idea how ridiculous we look?" she asked a minute later, darting a glance toward the Rolls. "Jogging in front of a Rolls Royce at five-thirty on a Saturday morning?"

He laughed softly. "We've done crazier things," he reminded her. "How about the night we walked home in the rain from Jones Hall after the concert and got soaked to the skin?"

"Or the time we overbalanced that little boat when we were fishing and fell into the lake, fully clothed?" She grinned. "We've had some good times together."

"They're not over, either," he replied. "Not by a long shot, Satin."

She stopped suddenly, fighting the nausea as she gazed up at him. She swallowed, breathing unsteadily. "John, I think I'm going to faint," she managed.

He caught her on her way to the sidewalk and lifted her easily in his hard arms. "Madeline, what's the matter?" he asked, his voice taut, concerned. "Madeline!"

"I . . . I just felt faint," she whispered, resting her head against his warm, broad chest, breathing in the male scent of his big body with a sense of homecoming. "A little sick . . ."

He muttered something that sounded like the worst kind of swear words, striding quickly toward the Rolls where Josito was holding the back door open.

"Drive until you run out of gas," he told Josito as he got into the back seat with Madeline on his lap. He closed the door, then the curtain between them and the front seat.

Josito got behind the wheel and minutes later they were under way.

"I thought you said that damned doctor gave you a clean bill of health," he growled down at her.

"He did," she said stubbornly. She drew an unsteady breath and relaxed against him, savoring his strength. "Don't fuss at me, John, I feel dreadful."

His arms tightened gently. "Want something cold to drink?" he asked. "A Coke? Something slushy with ice?"

She nuzzled against him. "Ice would be lovely."

"No sooner said than done." He moved, his arm stretching. "Josito, take us by that new ice-cream place."

"*Sí, señor.* Is the *señorita* okay?"

"I reckon," he growled.

"I really am," she murmured weakly. "Or I will be when I get my breath back. I just overdid it a little. I haven't jogged in a while, you know," she said, eager to convince him that it was nothing serious. John, being John, would think nothing of walking into any doctor's office he happened to come to and carrying her straight into an examination room. He had the arrogance of high position and great wealth, and he used it when he needed to.

"You're not going to do anything silly, are you?" she asked, thinking aloud. She eased her head back on his broad shoulder, staring uneasily up at his hard, lined face. "John, I'll be okay. I really will."

The lines didn't smooth out. His glittering silver eyes ran over her like loving hands searching for broken bones. "You scare me sometimes," he said enigmatically. His voice was husky, concerned.

She smiled. "I'm not trying to shoot the rapids, am I?" she laughed. "Or hang glide . . ."

"My God, shut up," he sighed roughly, leaning back against the seat and drawing her with him. "If you get sick just running, imagine how you'd feel soaring down some damned mountain? I haven't forgotten the day you decided to try parachuting," he added with a black glare.

She shifted uncomfortably and settled closer against his warm body. "I didn't put the tree in the way," she reminded him.

"It took me the better part of an hour to cut you loose," he grumbled. "After I spend a damned hour scouring the woods looking for you. You're lucky it took me that long."

She made a face at him. "Then you must have been in a nasty temper. You bawled me out as it was!"

"And it served you right, you little daredevil," he said unsympathetically. "Madeline, don't you even think about pulling anything that stupid now," he added in a challenging tone, his jaw set.

Her heart jumped. She tried to breathe normally while she stared into his hard eyes. Did he know more about her condition than he was letting on? She tried to recall some of the strange remarks he'd made to her lately.

"Not until you get over this damned virus," he added in a minute, and she relaxed unconsciously.

"They do... hang on," she murmured.

"I wish you'd see my doctor," he said. "I'm not sure I trust the one you went to."

"He *was* your doctor!"

"The company doctor," he agreed, "not my personal physician." He stared at her contemplatively. "Suppose I have them set up an appointment for you?"

"Oh, no, that won't be necessary," she said quickly. "I'll be just fine. See, I'm not even nauseated anymore," she assured him as she tried to sit up.

"Just stay where you are," he shot back, holding her. His eyes were suddenly level with her own, and she could feel his warm, smoky breath. "It's not that big a car. Suppose we had to pick up a stranded motorist or something—where would he sit if you moved and started taking up more space?"

She tried to resist a smile. "He? It might be a gorgeous buxom blonde, and then what would you do?"

He considered that, and the mustache twitched.

"I guess she'd have to sit on Josito's lap," he laughed softly.

She linked her hands around his neck. "Are you insinuating that I'm fat, Mr. Durango?" she murmured coyly.

He chuckled down at her. "Oh, no. Not fat." His hands found her thickening waist and pressed very gently, moving down to her hips and back up again, under the jogging shirt onto the bare skin of her back. "Not fat at all, Miss Vigny," he murmured, rubbing his nose provocatively against hers, the mustache almost touching her lips. "Just deliciously voluptuous."

"John, you promised," she reminded him as her pulse pounded wildly.

He grimaced, his hands stilling on her shoulder blades. "I guess I did," he admitted reluctantly. He brushed his mouth against her nose and then released her, easing her down to a sitting position beside him. "Feel better?"

"Yes and no," she murmured provocatively.

"You'd better stop right there, Satin, before you get in over your head," he told her. His eyes ran over her possessively. "God, you're lovely! You were always a knockout, but lately you're staggering."

She dropped her eyes to his open-necked shirt. "How you do go on, Mister John," she drawled, blinking her long eyelashes at him.

He smiled at her. "I guess I do." Then his expression became completely serious. "Honey, why won't you marry me? Won't you even think about it?"

She gazed up into his eyes and nodded slowly. "I—I'll think about it. But no more pressure tactics. Please. I have to make up my own mind about this. And I need a little time."

"Whatever you say, Satin," he murmured, drawing her close. "Whatever you say."

If only it had been that easy, she sighed, staring around her at the forest of roses. The scent was overpowering, and despite John's promise to stop pressuring her, they kept on coming every day.

She knew he thought he was giving her the time she'd asked for, so she made no protest. She couldn't expect him to change his ways overnight. But when she discovered that he was turning up in all the places she frequented, she put her foot down.

"You're following me," she accused late the next week when she "accidentally" bumped into him at a liquor store in one of the malls.

He drew her aside, away from the man behind the counter and his three customers, into an aisle stocked with wines. "What are you doing here?" he asked her, his voice lowered. "You shouldn't be drinking. I thought the virus gave you nausea?"

God alone knew of a virus that could last for weeks, but apparently John wasn't even suspicious about it, thank goodness.

"I'm not buying something to drink," she whispered. "I am getting a small bottle of rum with which to make a rum cake. I know how you like rum cakes, and they don't taste the same with artificial flavor."

He frowned thoughtfully down at her. "Well, I suppose most of the alcohol does evaporate—but get some coconut rum," he added. "If you use half that and half dark rum, you get an unforgettable cake."

She gasped. "How ever did you learn that?" she asked in her slowest drawl. "You don't know how to cook!"

"Josito told me," he said.

"Well, I won't argue with Josito," she said. "Coconut rum it is. Now why are you following me? You were at the grocery store—the grocery store, for Pete's sake!—and then yesterday you

were at the pharmacy. Today you're here....
John, I'm better, honestly I am."

"I know that," he grumbled. "You even look
better. But those damned things hang on. You
might feel dizzy again, and who'd look after
you?"

"Nobody would do it the way you do, and
that's a fact," she sighed, half-amused, half-
flattered. "I know you want to give me the time I
asked for, so you're watching over me without
actually making contact. But you really don't
have to go to these lengths, you see. You could
call me once in a while, you could have dinner
with me...."

"When?" he shot back. "Tonight? What shall
I bring?"

She couldn't help laughing. "All right, tonight
will be fine. You can bring a bottle of port to go
with the spaghetti and garlic bread."

"Are you going home now?" he asked.

"Oh, yes, sir, just as soon as I buy my rum,"
she agreed smartly.

"See that you do," he said, turning away.

She stuck out her tongue at his departing back.

Actually, she had good intentions about going
home. But she hadn't banked on having a flat tire
on the way.

"How could you do this to me?" she asked the little yellow car as she stared helplessly at its flat rear tire. "I rescued you from months of having to listen to that grinning salesman tell lies about you, from having total strangers feeling your upholstery. And you do *this* to me!"

She opened the hood with a sigh and got out the lug wrench and jack, and proceeded to try to figure out how to get the car off the ground. She actually had the jack put together and was sliding it under the little car when there was a screeching of brakes.

She knew before she turned who it was. Sure enough, the Ferrari was parked across the street and John was walking toward her as she straightened from her task.

"What the hell are you doing?" John bellowed at her, his good intentions apparently forgotten.

"I'm changing a tire, of course, what does it look like?" she asked haughtily, annoyed at his autocratic manner. "Do you suppose I like standing here looking like a fool?"

"I don't know, do you?" he countered, rolling up the sleeves of his white shirt. "Get out of the way. This is man's work."

"How dare you!" she burst out, flattening herself against the side of the car to prevent him from getting the jack. "This is not the Victorian age, mister, and you may own an oil company, but you don't own this car or me!"

"I'm going to," he said calmly. "Get out of the way."

"You are not!"

"You're going to marry me," he informed her. "And soon. I've had about as much of this waiting as I can stand. My nerves are raw from trying to watch out for you while you make up your mind."

"And what do you mean by that?" she demanded.

Across the street a crowd was gathering to watch the show.

"I mean you're driving me *nuts,* does that make it any clearer?"

Her eyebrows arched. "Who, me?"

"You!" His face hardened. "I can't eat, I can't sleep, I can't even do the job the stockholders expect me to do. My whole life is devoted to making sure you don't kill yourself!"

"How can jogging down a quiet street and buying a bottle of rum constitute suicide?" she asked with biting sarcasm.

"What would you call trying to change a flat tire in your condition!" he flung back, his eyes fiercely accusing.

She felt the blood slowly leaving her face. "What do you mean, *my condition?*"

He drew a deep breath, started to speak, and changed his mind. "I mean, my dear, you are just recovering from the flu," he ground out. "You don't have any business overexerting in this damned heat!"

She cocked her head at him, studying the hard, poker face that gave nothing away under its deep tan.

He sighed disgustedly. "Will you please move, your ladyship, or do I have to lift you out of the way?"

"I'd like to see you try," she challenged, knowing immediately that in his present state of mind it wasn't the thing to say.

He bent, lifting her before she had time to react, and cradled her against his chest as he crossed the street to where the Ferrari was parked.

"John Cameron Durango . . . !" she began.

He stopped at the passenger door of the sleek black car and bent his dark head to kiss the breath out of her, ignoring the small crowd of amused onlookers.

She didn't even struggle. The touch of his mouth was new, exciting, and she loved the feel of it against her own. The slow, sweet pressure drugged her senseless as the sun beat down on them.

He drew back a breath. "Still want to argue with me?" he whispered unsteadily.

"More than ever, if that's my punishment," she whispered back, parting her lips invitingly.

He chuckled softly. "Wait until I get you home, honey," he murmured. He set her down and opened the door. "Get in. I'll have someone come back for the VW."

"You're going to just leave it there?" she asked.

"Well, it isn't going to drive itself away," he pointed out.

Her lips pursed mutinously. "You might at least get my purse for me," she coaxed.

He looked up at the sky, his eyes pleading for strength. "All right," he muttered, starting back across the street.

"Man's work, is it?" she grumbled to herself, easing across the car into the driver's seat. "Driving him nuts, am I?" She leaned out the window as she started the powerful engine. "I'll leave your car in my driveway," she called sweetly. "You can trade me the VW for it!" And she roared away, leaving behind a giggling bunch of spectators and a bitterly cursing John Durango.

He knew. She was absolutely sure of it now. It explained his strange attitude recently, all the pampering, all the unexpected meetings. He knew about the baby, and that was why he was pressuring her to marry him. He wanted the child—and he wanted her, physically at least. No child of his was going to be born illegitimate, no sir. Damn the personal sacrifice. He had probably figured it was all his fault, anyway; he had that much of a sense of responsibility. He hadn't taken precautions, so it was up to him to take the consequences along with her.

She was crying bitterly when she got back to her house. She left the Ferrari in the driveway, with the keys in it, and ran inside and locked the door.

It seemed like hours before the tears stopped. At about the same time there came a furious knock on the front door.

She sat up on the sofa. "Go away!" she shouted tearfully.

"Open it or I'll break it down," came the taciturn reply. "Your choice."

A premonition about the repair bill decided her in a flash. She got to her feet quickly and, drying the tears with the back of her hand, opened the door.

John's eyes were blazing, his face stormy, but when he looked down at her sad little face, he softened visibly.

"I brought your car back." He handed her the keys. "Are you all right?"

That deep concern in his voice almost made her knees buckle, but she only nodded, determined to present a calm front. "Thank you."

He looked as if he wanted badly to say something but didn't exactly know how to start. He made a strange little gesture with one big hand.

"See you," he bit off, turning.

She stared tearfully at his broad back. He'd gone to all that trouble because he was worried about her, and she had repaid him by throwing pies in his face and leaving him to change a flat tire in the blazing sun. A sob worked its way out of her throat. He wasn't even going to blow up at her.

"John!"

He froze in his tracks, without turning. "Well?" he asked testily.

"Sup... supper's at seven," she blurted out.

There was a long pause, and she was afraid he wasn't even going to answer or, worse, refuse. "I'll be here," he said finally, and left without looking back at her.

She went back inside and closed the door. This wouldn't do. It just wouldn't do. He was so obviously upset, and it was her fault as much as his. She couldn't marry him. She couldn't. It wouldn't be fair to let him assume the burden of both her and the child just out of a misguided sense of responsibility. If he loved her, it would be different. Her eyes closed on a wave of anguish. If he loved her...!

But that was like wishing that grass would turn to silver with diamond dewdrops. She'd wondered why he wanted to marry her—now she knew. John felt guilty, that was all. And he'd always been fond of her. He wanted her. But none of that added up to love. And Madeline couldn't settle for anything less, not for a lifetime. A marriage that was entered into for any reason less than love on both sides automatically had two strikes against it. She worshipped the ground John Durango walked on, but unrequited love would eventually turn to ashes. The torment of loving and not being loved in return would kill her.

There was no longer any need for time to make up her mind. She had made her decision. It was far better for her, and for John, if they stopped seeing each other, and if she left Houston. That was what she was going to tell him tonight.

She spent the entire afternoon making a special spaghetti sauce, preparing a chef's salad and homemade garlic bread to go with it. And for dessert she made John the rum cake he loved.

It was nerve-wracking; she dreaded telling him her decision. But it would be for the best. She repeated that like a litany while she showered and rifled the closet for something to wear. The black dress was definitely out, unless she could slit it all the way down one side from breast to toe, and she hadn't bought another evening gown. So she decided to be casual and dressed in powder blue slacks with a pale blue patterned flowing cotton blouse. She left her hair long, because he liked it that way. Then she sat down and tried to find something to keep her busy until he arrived.

Time dragged horribly, and her own thoughts tormented her. These past weeks had taught her how much a part of her life John was. They'd taught her one more thing—that living without him was going to be nothing more than existing. The baby would compensate, of course. Her hands touched the slight swell of her stomach and she smiled. Oh, yes, the baby would compensate. She drifted off into a lazy daydream about John holding their soft little baby in his big arms.

She got out of the chair and went to make tea. That kind of thinking would get her nowhere. She had to be strong.

She opened the door at seven sharp, and found John on the doorstep with a bouquet of yellow and white daisies. Like Madeline, he'd opted for a casual suit of denim, expertly cut, with an open-necked, blue-patterned shirt.

"Read my mind, did you?" he asked, indicating her own casual outfit in a complementary shade of blue.

She laughed softly. "Looks like it, all right. What's the matter, did the florist run out of roses?" she asked, tongue-in-cheek, as he handed her the daisies.

He looked briefly uncomfortable. "Well, you said you were tired of them, didn't you?"

"I was. Thank you, John. I love daisies, too."

He lifted his head as he removed the Stetson and scowled. "What do I smell besides coconut?"

"Roses," she sighed, indicating the living room, which was a fragrant riot of vivid color.

He chuckled. "Overdid it, didn't I?" he asked.

She shook her head as she went off to find a container of some sort for the daisies. "A little. But I really did love them." In desperation, she pulled out a small vase and made a flower arrangement out of the daisies while he stood in the doorway and watched.

"Spaghetti, I believe you said?" he remarked. "Do I get to eat it this time, or are you planning to pour it in my lap again?"

"Just be thankful that you aren't getting a cream pie for dessert," she pointed out.

"Oh, hell, I forgot the wine," he said abruptly. "Want me to go out and get some?"

"No, that's all right," she said quickly, turning. "I'd just as soon have milk, myself, if you'll settle for coffee or iced tea."

"Suppose we both have milk?" he asked.

She eyed him coquettishly. "What a comedown."

He leaned against the doorjamb, watching her intently as she moved around the kitchen, setting the small table, laying out trivets, moving the spaghetti to the table, pouring the sauce.

"Be sure you don't miss anything," she chided gently. "Want to count my teeth?"

One corner of his mustache went up. "I like looking at you. Do you mind?"

She flushed like a young girl and bent to retrieve the garlic bread from the oven. When she had finished pouring milk into the glasses, she gestured for him to sit down.

"We could eat in the dining room, but it's so cluttered right now with my notes and drafts...."

"I kind of like the kitchen better," he admitted, seating her before he pulled out a chair and sat down next to her.

They ate in a strained silence. It wasn't like old times, when John would be telling stories about the oil company's early days, or about some of the places he visited on business. Or when she'd try out new plots and characters on him, to get his reaction. Now they seemed to have nothing to say; it was as if the pain of memory was lying heavy on them both.

When they finished—neither of them had shown any real appetite—Madeline led the way into the living room, leaving John to carry the coffee service on a tray. He set it down on the coffee table and plopped down next to Madeline on the sofa.

"Is this where you tell me you're leaving Houston?" he asked matter-of-factly, staying her hand as she reached for a cup.

She gaped at him. Her mouth fell open and she gasped at the unexpected question.

"That's what I thought," he sighed bitterly. "All this special treatment, right down to my favorite dessert: . . . Why the hell didn't you just come out with it? No guts?" he added with a cold smile.

She drew in a savage breath. "I've got plenty of guts," she shot back. "Why should I be afraid of you?"

"I'm a hell of a lot bigger than you are, for one thing," he reminded her.

"Big deal. The bigger they come, the harder they fall," she shot back, stiffening.

"I can't fall any harder than I already have," he said enigmatically. "If you leave Houston, I'll go with you," he added curtly.

She felt like grinding her teeth. "Will you be reasonable?" she burst out. "John, I've been taking care of myself for twenty-seven years! I've gotten very good at it!"

"You won't eat right," he growled, eyeing her. "You'll do stupid things like trying to change car tires in the heat of the day."

"I'll reform," she said stubbornly. "I'll practice not lifting handkerchiefs two hours a day."

He got up with a jerky motion and paced, fumbling to light a cigarette. "You could live at the ranch—I'd stay at the apartment. Josito could take care of you. You could have a maid, if you liked." He took a deep, defeated breath, his eyes empty as he looked down at her, taut and silent on the sofa. "Oh, God, why won't you marry me?" he ground out. "Have I managed to kill everything you felt for me?"

The look on his face made her hurt inside. Tears brimmed over in her eyes. She got to her feet and went to him, standing just in front of him, her hands going nervously to the front of his open-throated shirt.

"You know, don't you?" she whispered, her eyes wide with anxiety.

He put the cigarette in an ashtray beside him and straightened. His big hands went to her thickened waist and he drew her very gently against his big, warm body.

"I may be a man," he said softly, searching her eyes, "but I know a lot about these things. The fainting, the nausea—this . . . very attractive weight gain." He let his hands move lower, touching, hesitantly, the slight swell below her waist.

"And when you put two and two together...?" she prodded.

"I went crazy," he admitted, avoiding her eyes. "Absolutely crazy. I bought out half a toy store and hid the stuff in a closet at the apartment; I went to a bookstore and got everything they had on childbirth and being a parent. Then I sat down and tried to figure out how I was going to tell you that I knew—because you so obviously didn't want me to."

She toyed with a button on his shirt, her eyes closing wearily for an instant. "Because I was afraid you'd do exactly what you have done—insist on marrying me."

"We get along well together," he reminded her. "We always have, until lately. I could give the baby all the material advantages. I'd...care about him," he added helplessly. He moved suddenly, cupping her face in his hands to force her eyes up to his. "Tell me you want the baby," he whispered jerkily. "For God's sake, tell me that, even if you have to lie!"

He blurred in her vision. Tears rolled down her cheeks as she lifted her hand hesitantly to his crisp, dark hair, stroking it with a tenderness she hadn't felt in a long, long time. "Of course I want it," she whispered shakily. "Your child. Our child. I love you so much, how could I not want ... ?"

"Love me?" His voice sounded ragged. He stiffened against her, a shudder running through him. He drew her painfully close, wrapping her up, his restless eyes sliding over her, down to the soft swell of her breasts crushed against his massive chest. "Oh, God, if this is a dream, I don't ever want to wake up," he whispered. "Love— sweet, sweet love! A baby!" He buried his face hungrily in her soft throat. Something wet moistened her warm flesh as he cradled her in his arms, trembling. "Our baby... And you were going to walk out the door and vanish," he growled huskily, his voice accusing. "I would never have known what you really felt."

She muffled a sob against his shoulder. Her hands entwined behind his head, clinging. "I didn't want you to marry me because of the baby, because you felt it was your responsibility."

"My God, you don't know me at all, do you?" he mused. "In all my life I've never done a single thing unless it pleased me. And marrying you is damned sure going to fall into that category. You crazy woman, did you think it was only because of the baby? The baby is a bonus!"

Her heart threatened to burst with joy at the expression on his craggy face. "We should both have realized it would happen," he added gently. "That night we shared was too beautiful not to have borne fruit."

She smiled up at him, glowing. "What a very lovely way to put it."

He traced her soft mouth with a caressing finger. "I remember telling you before I carried you into my bedroom that I wanted to make love with you. And we did." He touched her rounded belly lightly, possessively, and smiled. "Love," he whispered.

She nuzzled her face into his shirt, feeling shy, embarrassed. He tipped her flushed face up to his gaze and smiled at the loving expression he found there. "Now," he said, "will you stop dumping spaghetti in my lap and throwing pies at me and stranding me in front of hysterical crowds?"

She went on tiptoe to brush her mouth against his. "If you'll stop trailing along behind me and burying me alive in roses," she agreed. She studied him solemnly. "Do you love me, John?" she asked quietly.

His eyes closed and opened again. "I've never said the words," he admitted curtly. "Not in my life. Not to Ellen, not to my father. It goes all the way back to the way I grew up, I reckon," he laughed shortly, making a joke of it. "But, my God, I feel it when I look at you; when I touch you." He lifted her in his hard arms and started toward the couch with her. "I can't tell you," he whispered hungrily, "not . . . just yet. But I can show you." He bent, brushing his mouth against hers. "I can show you."

He eased her onto the soft cushions, following her down, his body pressed intimately against hers. She felt his fingers slowly undoing the blouse down to her waist and she remembered as his head bent to her rosy breast that she hadn't bothered with a bra.

"John . . ." she whispered as his mouth trespassed on warm, swelling flesh.

It was different between them now. There was a new tenderness in the way he kissed her. The way he held her. It was as different from physical passion as water is from stone. There was a reverence in it that took her breath.

Her fingers, trembling, eager, opened his shirt to the waist and ventured inside, hungry to touch the firm muscles, to tangle in the thick covering of hair over them. Her mouth escaped his and pressed against his chest. She breathed in his scent as her lips explored the hard, warm, faintly damp contours. He lay back, letting her be aggressive for the first time, watching her quietly while she learned new things about his bronzed torso, about his reactions to her caresses.

"Men . . . like to be touched, too, don't they?" she asked after a minute, drawing back to look into his soft, loving eyes.

His mustache curled. "It depends on who's doing the touching," he informed her. "You touch me and it's the Fourth of July. I go up in flames."

He looked so devastatingly masculine like this, his mouth sensuous, a look in his eyes that made her body melt against him. The curling thick hairs on his chest tickled her bareness. He stiffened convulsively at the contact and caught his breath.

Her hands framed his rugged face and she smiled. "I like this, don't you?" she murmured, peeking at him through her lashes.

"If you keep this up," he replied unsteadily, "you may find yourself in deep trouble!"

She laughed softly, loving him with all her heart. Her fingers traced the hard lines of his face, the deep slow curve of his mouth. "May I ask you something very personal?'' she murmured.

"What?"

"Did you sleep with Melody?" She had to know. It was like slow poison inside her.

"No," he replied, and the truth of it was in his eyes. "Don't you know that I don't want anyone but you? Couldn't you tell that night we spent together that it had been a long time for me?"

"I thought it had, but I don't know a lot about men," she reminded him.

"I haven't touched another woman since the night I picked you up off the street in the rain," he said softly. His eyes caressed her, touched her, possessed her. "You've been an obsession with me since the beginning, and you've never known it. I've never let you know it," he corrected. "You were so damned vulnerable at first. And then, before I knew it, you'd put that burden of absolute trust on me, and my hands were truly tied. Until the night Elise gave that party," he added, smiling wickedly, "and you looked at me as if you'd kill to have my mouth on yours."

She drew in her breath. "I didn't realize," she said faintly.

"And you were so obviously jealous of Melody." He grinned. "That was encouraging."

"I'll just bet!"

"It was the opening I'd been looking for, and I took it. Then, when I made that first blatant pass, you took off like a scalded cat, and I was so afraid I'd ruined it all," he sighed.

"You frightened me," she admitted. "I'd never thought of you as a lover until then." She flushed softly. "I'd never been kissed like that, not even . . . it made me burn all over. But then, when you didn't call, I was afraid you didn't want to be friends anymore. I hemmed and hawed around for days and when I couldn't stand it anymore, I called and asked Josito where to find you." She smiled at him lazily. "I hoped you'd take the beer as a peace offering."

"I took more than the beer, if you'll remember," he murmured, drawing her mouth down onto his in a slow, sweet kiss.

"Why were you ashamed of the night we made love?" he asked gently. "Were you afraid I'd think you were easy?"

"Yes," she admitted. "I thought by giving in, I'd just joined the ranks of your other conquests."

"You crazy woman," he murmured, drawing a strand of her red gold hair across his throat. "I've told you, there were no other conquests."

"But you let me think there were. And you were horrible to me when I went to stay at Donald's," she reminded him.

He sighed, his eyes pained at the memory. "All I could think of was that you'd hated what happened, and that you were paying me back. You see, Ellen..." He touched her hair. "When Ellen lost her temper with me, she always ran to Donald," he said, surprising her by saying his cousin's name. "I don't think she ever let him touch her, don't misunderstand me. But Donald was always there when she needed a shoulder to cry on. It did terrible things to me. After a while, I hated them both. When she died, and he went to pieces at the funeral, a lot of things made sense. I shouldn't have married her. She was Donald's girl, you know. I should have realized that what I felt for her was infatuation, not something permanent. But by the time I did, it was too late. She had fallen in love with me and I felt responsible for her. But she wanted more than I was able to give her, and that's my cross."

She touched his cheek. "Donald never touched me," she said gently. "I couldn't have let anyone else, not after you."

"I should have known that, shouldn't I?" he asked, his voice rich and deep, velvety and full of wonder. "But I had some crazy idea that you preferred Donald." He sighed deeply. "Let's face it, love, I'm far from perfect. I've got a hell of a temper and I'm not easy to get along with even on my good days. Donald is mischievous, even-tempered...."

"Very nice and unassuming, and as different from you as night is from day," she continued. She bent down and brushed her mouth over his. "Then why is it that I still prefer you?"

He eased her across him and his mouth bit hungrily into hers, the kiss so deep and ardent that she shuddered, moaning softly.

"I want you so," he whispered shakily, gazing into her rapt eyes. "In every way there is."

She laughed. "In a few months, I'll look like a pumpkin and two cantaloupes. We'll see how you like me then," she challenged.

"You're carrying my child," he said, his eyes dropping caressingly to her stomach. "I'd like you if you looked like a blimp."

"I probably will."

"You don't sound too unhappy at the prospect," he chuckled.

She shook her head. "I'm not unhappy at all. I like being pregnant."

"You don't feel . . . trapped?" he asked, concern in his face, his eyes.

"Oh, no," she assured him. "Funny, I always thought of any kind of commitment as a padlock on my freedom. But the baby. . ." She smiled. "I've been thinking up names. If he's a boy, I'd like to call him Cameron Edward. . . ."

"How about Candy for a girl?" he replied.

"Done!"

He laughed wickedly. "And if they're twins?"

Her eyes lit up. "John, there are twins on my side of the family, at least three sets that I know of."

He sighed. "Mine, too, honey. It was way back, but definitely twins."

"You're not sorry about the baby, are you?" she asked, worried.

"My God, are you blind?" he asked, one corner of his mouth plunging.

"Just checking."

"We'd better start thinking about dates, places, and witnesses," he observed. "Before very much longer, you're going to be obviously pregnant, and I don't want any snide remarks made about my wife."

"I'd like a church wedding," she said definitely. "But a very small one, okay?"

"Okay." He twined a long strand of her hair around one finger as he propped himself on an elbow to look down at her pink bareness, feasting on the sight. "God, you're pretty," he murmured.

She couldn't help the blush. This was still new territory and she lowered her eyes to his hair-matted chest. "Lecherous thing," she accused coyly. "Getting girls in trouble . . ."

"You helped me," he reminded her with a wicked grin.

"Temporary insanity," she pleaded. "I wasn't responsible."

He chuckled, bending to brush his mouth over her soft skin with devastating tenderness. "Liar," he whispered, the mustache tickling.

She smoothed the cool, dark strands of hair at his nape, drowning in the sweetness of his mouth as it touched her. "I love you," she whispered shakily, her eyes closing. "You're my best friend in the whole world, John Durango."

He lifted his head, catching her eyes to read their misty green depths. "You need to hear it, don't you?" he asked softly. "Women need the words."

She managed a smile for him. "I can see it," she corrected, searching his face, awed at the tenderness, the soft hunger in it.

He drew in a steadying breath, tracing her mouth with his finger. "I . . . do love you," he ground out. "I always will." He nuzzled his forehead against hers, his eyes closing for a minute. They opened and looked directly into hers. "There'll never be another woman."

"Or another man for me," she promised, loving him with her eyes. "I've been so lonely without you. . . ."

He kissed her eyes closed, whisper movements of his lips brushing her eyelids, her wet lashes. His body moved, easing gently down over hers, his arms catching the bulk of his weight as his mouth poised a breath away from her waiting lips.

"Now it's your turn," he murmured deeply. "Suppose you show me how lonely it's been."

"I'd love to," she murmured, smiling as she reached up to bring his head down. She drowned in the sweetness of the long, slow kiss, loving the weight and warmth of his big body, the closeness. She was fighting for breath when he finally drew away.

"The baby . . . !" he whispered suddenly, starting to lift away.

But her arms held him, tender, wanting arms. "You won't hurt the baby," she promised with a warm smile. "I asked the doctor," she added with a twinkle in her soft eyes. Suddenly she laughed. "John, can you imagine what Elise is going to think?"

He chuckled softly. "If we'd had any idea what was coming, I'd have had you grab your side and fake an attack of appendicitis. My God, and I told you that you could name it after me . . . !"

She buried her face in his warm throat. "The joke was on us, my darling," she whispered.

He stiffened, drawing back to look down at her. "Say that again," he breathed unsteadily, watching her mouth.

The smile faded. "My darling," she whispered obligingly.

He bent, and his mouth parted hers with exquisite slowness, and he eased down again, letting his broad, warm chest melt onto the soft bareness of hers in the silence of the living room.

She felt the tremor go through him, took his craggy face in her hands to ease it away from hers and looked up into his fiery silver eyes.

"So you're going to marry me?" he asked roughly.

"I think I'm going to have to," she whispered unsteadily, feeling her body's instant response to his. "There's just one thing, though," she added with a last, faint flare-up of mischief.

"What?" he asked.

She ran her fingers into the thick hair over his ears. "I won't sleep in the bunkhouse with the ten-foot snakes," she whispered.

He chuckled softly, bending. "No, you won't," he murmured against her soft mouth. "You'll sleep with me. And I'll keep you safe through the night, every night, as long as we live."

She reached up to draw him down against her. "We'll live forever," she promised him, "because that's how long I'll love you...."

Next door, Miss Rose saw the lights in Madeline's house go off, and her twinkling eyes caught a glimpse of the Ferrari still parked in the driveway. As she closed her curtains with a wistful smile, she already had her busy mind at work on a proper wedding gift.

Take 3 of
"The Best of the Best™"
Novels FREE
Plus get a FREE surprise gift!

Special Limited-time Offer

Mail to The Best of the Best™

**3010 Walden Avenue
P.O. Box 1867
Buffalo, N.Y. 14269-1867**

YES! Please send me 3 free novels and my free surprise gift. Then send me 3 of "The Best of the Best™" novels each month. I'll receive the best books by the world's hottest romance authors. Bill me at the low price of $3.74 each plus 25¢ delivery and applicable sales tax, if any.* That's the complete price and a savings of over 10% off the cover prices—quite a bargain! I understand that accepting the books and gift places me under no obligation ever to buy any books. I can always return a shipment and cancel at any time. Even if I never buy another book from Harlequin, the 3 free books and the surprise gift are mine to keep forever.

183 BPA ANV9

Name	(PLEASE PRINT)
Address	Apt. No.
City	State Zip

This offer is limited to one order per household and not valid to current subscribers.
*Terms and prices are subject to change without notice. Sales tax applicable in N.Y.
All orders subject to approval.

UBOB-295   ©1990 Harlequin Enterprises Limited

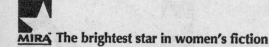

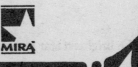